Molly Black

Bestselling author Molly Black is author of the MAYA GRAY FBI suspense thriller series, comprising nine books (and counting); of the RYLIE WOLF FBI suspense thriller series, comprising six books (and counting); of the TAYLOR SAGE FBI suspense thriller series, comprising six books (and counting); and of the KATIE WINTER FBI suspense thriller series, comprising nine books (and counting).

An avid reader and lifelong fan of the mystery and thriller genres, Molly loves to hear from you, so please feel free to visit www.mollyblackauthor.com to learn more and stay in touch.

ISBN: 978-1-0943-9518-0

BOOKS BY MOLLY BLACK

MAYA GRAY MYSTERY SERIES
GIRL ONE: MURDER (Book #1)
GIRL TWO: TAKEN (Book #2)
GIRL THREE: TRAPPED (Book #3)
GIRL FOUR: LURED (Book #4)
GIRL FIVE: BOUND (Book #5)
GIRL SIX: FORSAKEN (Book #6)
GIRL SEVEN: CRAVED (Book #7)
GIRL EIGHT: HUNTED (Book #8)
GIRL NINE: GONE (Book #9)

RYLIE WOLF FBI SUSPENSE THRILLER
FOUND YOU (Book #1)
CAUGHT YOU (Book #2)
SEE YOU (Book #3)
WANT YOU (Book #4)
TAKE YOU (Book #5)
DARE YOU (Book #6)

TAYLOR SAGE FBI SUSPENSE THRILLER
DON'T LOOK (Book #1)
DON'T BREATHE (Book #2)
DON'T RUN (Book #3)
DON'T FLINCH (Book #4)
DON'T REMEMBER (Book #5)
DON'T TELL (Book #6)

KATIE WINTER FBI SUSPENSE THRILLER
SAVE ME (Book #1)
REACH ME (Book #2)
HIDE ME (Book #3)
BELIEVE ME (Book #4)
HELP ME (Book #5)
FORGET ME (Book #6)
HOLD ME (Book #7)
PROTECT ME (Book #8)
REMEMBER ME (Book #9)

PROLOGUE

Lottie Jones was having a really hard night.

The second she'd caught her boyfriend, George—now her *ex-boyfriend*—in their bed with another hussy from his favorite watering hole, the Rusty Nail, she'd walked out, fully intending to never look back.

Rotten bastard. That had been the second time in as many months that he'd cheated, and she was determined to make sure there wasn't a third. *Fool me once...*

Now, as she walked along the shoulder of Interstate 86, all of her belongings—at least, she thought it was all of them, but she'd been in too much of a rush, tripping through their bedroom in the dark—in a backpack slung over her shoulder, she decided this was for the best.

George was holding her back. She'd wanted him to take her east. *Begged* him, especially when she heard of all the opportunities in Indiana for good waitresses. That was what her friend Millie had told her when she'd called Lottie from Indianapolis. There were opportunities everywhere, it seemed—a labor shortage. Now, she had the chance to make some serious money and get a better place than that old, broken-down trailer.

So what if she didn't have the car? The money? A place to stay? Anything was better than being with that two-timer. She'd sleep in a tree to get away from him.

As she walked, her phone lit up with a text. Funny, she hadn't expected there'd be reception out here in the middle of nowhere. *Baby, come home.*

She snorted. Right. It was after two in the morning, and she was exhausted after a long shift at the Waffle House. But she'd walk over hot coals to get away from that jerk. She was *that* determined now.

Baby, I'm sorry. It won't happen again.

Yeah. That's what he'd said the last time. She opened up her phone, deleted the messages, blocked him, and scrubbed his number and picture from her phone, feeling powerful for the first time. She regretted the fact that even though she'd deleted his number, she still had it committed to memory. But she guessed it served her right, for wasting five years of her life with him.

That's a useless bit of information to have. Because I'm never calling or texting him again, she thought, turning her phone off. It was almost dead, and she needed to save the battery for important things. Just in case.

Headlights shone behind her, painting a long, thin shadow of her form on the gravel shoulder ahead. Not many people out at this hour of night, and even fewer willing to pick up a hitchhiker on this road, nicknamed the Highway Thru Hell. It was desolate, for sure, so barren and impossibly large, with only the occasional run-down, one-horse town. People who lived in this area of the world, at best, wanted to be left alone, and at worst, harbored some deep-seated resentment of others. Left to fester long enough, that turned into rage, and sometimes violence. Lottie didn't care much about the rumors of murders and kidnappings along this road—as far as she was concerned, the Highway Thru Hell led right to George's doorstep. Anything was better than that.

She spun, squinting in the bright, square headlights coming near, and jogged backwards in her cowboy boots and short skirt, sticking her thumb out.

The vehicle, a family SUV, whizzed by without stopping.

"Screw you, can't help a girl in need, huh?" she snarled, shaking a fist at the red taillights as they sped away from her. California plates, of course. Losers.

A few steps later, a sign appeared on the side of the road. BEARMOUTH REST AREA 5 MILES.

She groaned. She'd already been walking for what felt like ages. Five miles? Would she even make it?

And what would be there when she got there? Bearmouth wasn't exactly a thriving center of industry. She'd likely find nothing more than crappy coffee and a hard bench to spend the night on. Hooray. Her forty-year-old bones ached at the thought.

For the first time, she felt a pang of regret. *Maybe I should've given him another chance.*

No. No, this was right. She needed to stick to her guns. Someone would come along eventually. She had a few dollars in her purse, from that evening's tips. Maybe someone would drive her all the way out to the next motel. Or even just let her sleep in the passenger seat. She had to keep going, had to get as far away from George as she could, until the option of turning around wasn't possible.

It was just as she'd resolved to do so that the headlights of another car appeared behind her.

She spun, and, as before, extended her arm, holding her thumb out so it wouldn't be missed.

It was a small car, a sportscar, headlights low to the ground. At first, she thought it'd just speed right past her. But before it did, it suddenly slowed, then the brake lights went on, and it pulled to the shoulder up ahead.

She pumped her fist in celebration and ran to catch up to the car. She wasn't one to know the models and makes, but it was an old-model car, blue. Nice. She imagined the person who drove it must collect them. The passenger-side window was half-down, and she ducked to peer inside.

"Hey, baby. You goin' somewhere?" a gravelly voice said.

The cabin was dark, but it didn't take much to tell that this man was an utter creep. His face was cloaked in shadow, so all she could see were two thick hands gripping the steering wheel. She couldn't see his eyes, but she knew they were leering at her.

"Uh…" she stammered. Better than nothing. She could at least get a ride to the next stop. "Yes, I was looking for a ride up to the next exit."

"That all?"

She put a hand on the metal door handle. "Well… we'll see. How far are you going?"

He chuckled, low. "I'm goin' all the way. I think you should come, too."

Her stomach turned. Sex jokes already. She straightened and looked down the road, just as another car went past. During her years working at the diner, she'd learned to spot a creep. And this one was Grade A. All sorts of red flags were going up.

He reached over to open the door for her. "Come on in, baby. Keep me company. It's getting cold out there. You need someone to keep you warm?"

She stepped back. "On second thought, I think I'll just keep walking."

"I scared you away, huh?" He laughed.

He found this funny? Bastard. Just like George, always laughing at the wrong things. "Yeah, you did." She waved at him. "Thanks, but no thanks."

He simply shrugged, straightened behind the wheel, shifted into drive, and took off.

She stood there, watching his taillights disappear around a bend, and sighed. If he'd really been one of those kidnappers or murderers, he probably wouldn't have given up so easily.

And now here she was, completely out of luck.

Lottie turned and searched down the stretch of road, desperately willing another car to come by. Her cowboy boots were well broken in—she'd had them since high school—but it didn't help. Her feet ached more than ever.

And now, even worse, she had to pee.

She hadn't thought about that particular problem until just now. Scanning the area, she sighed. She couldn't just drop trousers on the shoulder. With her luck, that would be when a whole slew of cars came down the highway, catching her in the act.

So Lottie went to the very edge of the road and peered into the darkness, over a low fence. It seemed fairly level there. A field. Hopefully there'd be no bears or bison or wolves to bother her. She could just go a few yards out, crouch in the grass, and get it over with. A minute, tops.

Taking a deep breath, she straddled the fence. It was quite a bit steeper than she'd thought, and the soles of her boots were worn flat, so she stumbled and slid down a sharp embankment as she made her way in the darkness on the other side. The moonlight illuminated the tall grass, which slapped at her bare knees.

After a few feet, she stopped, pulled her underwear down, crouched, and relieved herself.

When she was done, she pulled up her panties and started back toward the road, noticing a more level path in the moonlight. She took that one instead.

But as she neared the road, she saw something glowing in the moonlight. It looked like the shining mane of a white horse, lying motionless on its side.

As she neared it, though, she saw other features. Human features. A naked leg. An arm. A face.

It was a girl, lying on her back, her blonde hair splayed out around her, legs and arms unnaturally posed. She'd been dumped there, and she was undoubtedly dead.

Lottie let out a little scream, her knees buckling as she hurried to make the rest of the trip back to the road.

And then Lottie did the only thing she could think to do.

She turned on her phone and called that bastard, George.

CHAPTER ONE

FBI agent Rylie Wolf sat in her office at the Rapid City Headquarters, staring at the files and thinking about the conversation she'd had with her partner, Michael Brisbane.

"Okay, what is up with you? I mention dinner and you don't jump all over that like a rabid dog? Are you feeling all right?"

He nodded. "Yeah, but Wolf..."

From the look on his face, she could tell it was something serious. "What is it?"

"Well... look. It's like this," he said, taking a deep breath. "What I said before about your sister was cruel and said in the heat of the moment. I didn't mean it. And of course, if I can, I want to help you find out what happened to her."

She smiled. "Oh. Well, I appreciate that. But don't worry. I get the feeling you might be right. That it's too far in the past, and it'll be impossible to uncover anything new. So maybe—"

"But that's the thing," he said, swallowing hard.

She stopped. "What's the thing?"

"I went in to the office today, and I thought I'd look into it on my lunch break. And you know, the new field office has an entire room of cold case files pertaining to this area, from all the other offices, that are sitting there in boxes. There are so many of them, it'll take ages to go through, because they're from years and years past, and they're not in any order. It's like the field offices just threw them together and shipped them off to us, to let us worry about them. Anyway, there was a bunch of stuff that was miscategorized and put in the wrong box, and this afternoon, I found it..."

He was babbling now, a mile a minute, and she wasn't quite sure what he was saying. "Do you mean you found something pertaining to my case?"

He nodded and reached into his pocket, pulling out a thin, golden chain. Dangling from it was a small M in fancy script.

A sense of déjà vu flooded her. She hadn't thought of that necklace in decades. But the second she saw it, she knew exactly where she'd seen it last.

On Maren's neck, the night before she'd disappeared.

"Where did you get that?" she whispered, unable to take her eyes off it.

He reached for a chair to the dining set and pulled it out for her. "I think you and I had better sit down and talk about this."

She nodded, stumbling to the kitchen table and sitting down, feeling strange and weightless, like she was watching this happen to somebody else.

"I found it in an envelope. There wasn't much. Just a slip of paper that said it was found in Elephant Hole Well. That's all."

Elephant Hole. That wasn't far from Story Creek, the RV park where they'd been staying when two strangers arrived, killed everyone at their campsite, and left with her older sister, who was just twelve at the time.

"There has to be more. Who found it? Was it near anything? What—"

He held up his hands. "I don't know. I'm only telling you what I found."

"Well, I need to look at it. Show me the box where you got it from." She stood up. Maybe there was more evidence. Something Michael had overlooked.

"I was afraid you'd say that," he said, standing and following her out the door.

Now, as she stared into the box, that familiar feeling of defeat crowded in. She'd spent six hours going over every last shred of evidence in the box. Michael had been right. It was a mishmash of stuff, terribly labeled and in no particular order. He'd been helping her, but even he'd had to go. It was after one in the morning now. He'd urged her to give it up, but she couldn't.

After all this time, she had something new.

Shoving the box of odds and ends away, she turned on her computer and Googled Elephant Hole. Just as she'd thought, it wasn't very far from where Maren had disappeared. A mile east. So that meant Maren had been taken east.

To where?

It was the smallest crumb of information. But it was better than anything she'd gotten in the past decades.

Though she'd just gotten back to town after the last big case, she couldn't stay here and expect to forget that. Not now. Not knowing that there was a new lead in the case of her sister, who was now missing almost thirty years.

As she was sitting there, her phone rang. She looked at the display. Cooper Rich, her friend from the Seattle Field Office. He'd been calling her all evening, but every time he rang, she let it go to voicemail. Needing a friendly voice after weeding through such morbid files, she picked up. "Hey, Coop."

"Hey, you. You avoiding me?"

She smiled. She and Coop had always flirted about, but never really gotten past a little bit of romantic tension. Bad timing. She was queen of that. "No. Just busy."

"How you feeling? You had it pretty bad there for a while."

"Oh, ship-shape. Everything's on the mend. How are you? You said in your last message you had something to tell me?"

"Ah. So you did get my messages? And you weren't the least bit curious what I had to say? Left Seattle behind for good, have you?"

She let out a short laugh. "No, I just really don't care if Bill Matthews gets another award from his daddy."

Bill Matthews was the special agent in charge of the Seattle unit, the man who basically sent her packing to the middle of the country just because he didn't like her. Probably her fault for publicly telling him off one too many times, but the guy was a jerk. Matthews, the idiot with no real-world skills to be in the FBI, had gotten where he was by simple nepotism, and his high-ranking father always shielded him from any negative publicity.

"It's not that," Rich said, his voice low.

"Uh-oh. That sounds bad," she murmured, wondering what on earth this could be about. She'd long since stopped caring about what was happening in Seattle. Ever since they declared they were done with her, she said the same of them, and meant it. Matthews may have hated her, but now he couldn't touch her.

"Matthews is advancing some complaints about you to Jerry."

She frowned. Jerry Matthews was the deputy director, and Bill's father. He was a more sensible guy than Bill, but he still propped his son up, even though the man had no idea how to run a washing machine, much less an entire department in the FBI. "Complaints?"

"Yeah. Big ones. Remember Moses Bedelbaum?"

She snorted. Of course she remembered that guy. Posed as a mild-mannered English teacher in a downtown Seattle school, but apparently that hadn't paid enough. He'd gotten into selling drugs to students, then used those drugs to ply some of the female students and deliver them into the sex trade. The guy had been defiant, adamantly professing his innocence even while boxfuls of evidence were being pulled out of his apartment. She'd been pissed at him, yes, because one of the theories around Maren had been that she, too, had been delivered into sex slavery. She'd slammed the butt of her pistol into his face, giving him a killer black eye, but she hadn't felt a single day's remorse over the fact. That trash deserved it.

"What are you saying?"

"I know, it's bullshit, but—"

"Just tell me what it is, Coop." She didn't have time for this.

"All right, all right. His case is coming up and there are a few other complaints, and they think it could spell trouble for you."

She sighed. "Fine. Bring it."

"You don't care?"

She laughed mirthlessly. "Am I supposed to? Of course I'll care if anything comes of it. But right now, I'm going to keep doing my job." Something suddenly struck her. "So let me guess. Bill called you into his office and told you all this, right?"

"Yeah."

She gritted her teeth. That was so *like* him, the scumbag. "You know why? I bet you he's hoping I crawl into my little hole and go away. He read about the last case I was involved in and he knows he hasn't beaten me. He wanted you to tell me, because he hoped it'd shut me up and get me to play nice. Well, you can tell him to go screw himself."

"You think?"

"Coop. I know. That's how he operates." She looked around at the pile of files around her. "Look, I've got to go. Big case I'm working on. And I have to find a way to make waves with it."

"Wolf…" His voice was a warning.

"Kidding. Bye, Coop, thanks for the info," she said, ending the call.

But really, she wasn't kidding. If Bill Matthews wasn't going to let her go, she'd have to find a way to make him rue the day he ever thought he could play against her. He wanted her to go away silently? She'd find a way to make the loudest noise she could.

Somehow.

She powered off the computer. She'd have to wait for the morning, but once the sun came up, she'd call her supervisor, explain the situation, and head out. *Elephant Hole, here I come.*

CHAPTER TWO

Rylie's home in Rapid City wasn't really a home. Though she'd been living there a couple of months after moving from the Seattle field office, she'd been on the road more than she'd been in town. Her apartment showed the obvious lack of care and flair. Though she'd been trying to spruce it up with a fresh coat of paint last night, renovations were now the last thing on her mind.

The moment she got out of bed, she packed for the drive back west. She hadn't even had a chance to put the clean clothes in the dresser yet, after washing them upon her return from Montana. They went straight from the laundry basket back into her duffel bag.

When she finished, it was eight in the morning, and she tapped her fingers on the kitchen counter as she filled a travel mug with fresh coffee, antsy to get on the road.

Her supervisor, Special Agent in Charge Kit Brandon, probably wouldn't be in yet, but no matter. Rylie had won a lot of brownie points, solving the past few murder cases, and Kit was always telling her she should put the brakes on and stop working so hard. She'd cut her some slack.

So when the phone rang to Kit's voicemail, Rylie said, "Hey, Kit, just wanted to let you know I'm taking the next few days off and going out of town for personal reasons. But call me if you need me. I'm around and can come right back."

She ended the call, hoisted her bag onto her shoulder, grabbed her commuter cup, and opened the front door—

—only to almost walk straight into the broad chest of her partner, Michael Brisbane. Movie star handsome and oddly happy-go-lucky for this line of work, he stared at her with his ice-blue eyes wide. "I knew it."

"What?" she asked innocently, not meeting those baby blue eyes of his, which could pour on the guilt trip better than anyone else she knew.

"Don't give me that. You know what," he said, eyeing her duffel bag. From the look of him, he hadn't slept very well. His clothes were uncharacteristically rumpled, and he had a shadow of dark stubble on his chin. "Let me guess. You're going to Elephant Butt."

"Elephant Hole," she corrected. "And I'm not going there. I'm going back to—"

"To Seattle?" He raised an eyebrow, his voice dripping with doubt. "I thought you didn't have anything there to go back to."

She couldn't meet his eyes. She stared just to the left of his ear as she formulated the lie. "No. I told you. I have a friend—he's like an uncle. Hal. He lives all alone on that ranch in Montana, and he seemed lonely when I stopped by before. And I'm trying to patch things up with my dad, too. So I thought I'd start in Cody and—"

"Whatever." He didn't buy a word of it.

"It's true—"

"Don't insult me, Wolf." He shook his head, his disappointment heavy in his face. She couldn't help feeling bad, and it wasn't just those big puppy-dog eyes of his. "It's our business to see through lies. And you're telling a doozy. You're probably the worst liar I've ever come across."

She shrugged. "Okay, I admit it. I just called Kit and left a message. I'll be back in a few days. I promise."

He dug his hand deep into the pocket of his slacks and flashed her a dark, hurt look. "And were you ever going to tell your partner?"

The truth was, she'd been thinking about it. He'd made the discovery of the necklace, after all. And though they'd only known each other over the span of a couple of months, during the last few cases, she'd come to trust him. "Sorry. But it has nothing to do with you, Bris. It's a personal thing, and I don't need a sidekick to come along with me on personal things, Robin—"

"For the last time, *I'm* Batman. You're the sidekick."

She glared at him. "Okay, have it your way. The bottom line is, I don't need your help. This is personal."

"But I found the necklace."

"So?"

"And so you were just going to jet out of here and leave me wondering where the hell you went? Is that it?" He leaned against the door jamb. "Nice. Now I see why you always worked alone."

She sighed. They'd been in some tight spots together over the last couple months, and he'd proven himself to be a regular prince, in more ways than one. Not only was he brave and trustworthy, but he was *damn* handsome, and as goofy as he could sometimes be, he had an easy, self-deprecating charm that people couldn't help but like. Everyone liked him.

Sometimes, she'd look at Michael Brisbane and get a feeling she hadn't had, even with her ex, Joe. Fluttery feelings that she had no business having where her partner was concerned.

And that was the last thing she needed.

"I'm sorry. Really. But I have to do this on my own. Please understand," she said, taking a step forward so he'd move aside and let her pass.

He didn't, and she found herself standing uncomfortably close to him. So close that if she took another step, she'd be standing on his toes. She expected him to move, but he didn't. Looking up, she met his eyes. Their gazes locked and he didn't flinch.

"Do you mind?"

"You know the answer to that," he murmured, staring her down. "If I didn't, I wouldn't be here."

She frowned. This was new to her. Where everyone liked Bris, not many people could stand Rylie. She knew that. She was difficult. It didn't just shock her that he actually wanted to spend time with her—it was a new experience. And as much as she would've liked the help and the company, she knew it was probably not a good idea. "Bris..."

"The least you can do is have breakfast before you hit the road," he said, bringing his arm from behind his back and holding up a white bakery bag. "Donuts. Come on."

Rylie sighed. She was kind of hungry, and it would be a hassle to have to stop at some fast-food restaurant or greasy spoon on the way. She stepped aside and let him in, grunting as if he wasn't doing her a favor.

"All right. Fine." She wagged a finger as he went to walk toward the table. "But don't think this is going to convince me to let you come with me."

He smiled, revealing those two adorable dimples. "Who me? Never." He bit into a donut, and powdered sugar puffed out in a cloud around his mouth. "You like jelly?"

"Fine." She sat down next to him and opened the bag, fishing a donut out. Anything was better than having to stop on the Highway Thru Hell, as their beat across several states in the northern part of the country was known. The more she'd gotten to know about the many crimes that took place along that stretch of interstate, the creepier it got. Murders, kidnappings, rapes... it wasn't safe at all.

"So," he said, polishing off his donut before she'd even taken a nibble of hers, "I'm assuming you found out more when you went through the files last night?"

She shook her head. "No. I didn't find anything else."

"So you're just going to go out to Elephant Butt—"

"Hole," she muttered. He was just being funny now.

"Right. Like I said. Elephant Hole. You're just going to go on a fishing expedition? Do cartwheels all over that place? It's an encampment, you know. A bunch of natives and soldiers had a few bloody run-ins there, or so the history books say."

"Of course I know. I used to live around there."

"So what do you expect you'll find, other than some old arrowheads?"

She shrugged and licked powdered sugar off her fingers. "I don't know. But I know that the place it was found was a mile east of the RV park in Story Creek where my sister was kidnapped. So it stands to reason that they took her that way, and stopped there, for whatever reason."

His eyes narrowed. "Wow. So you have it narrowed down to… like… half the country. That's helpful."

"Not half the country. There's a well there. And maybe there are more clues."

"After twenty years?"

Rylie grimaced at him, but she had to admit, he did have a point. It probably was a fool's hope. "You don't get it. When she disappeared, it was without a trace. That necklace is more information to go on than I've had—ever. So the least I can do is ask around Elephant Hole, make some inquiries, see if anyone remembers anything."

"From twenty years ago," he filled in.

He didn't have to tell her that. She knew her chances were slim. But she simply crumpled up the napkin and said, "I still have to do it."

"I know you do." He took another donut out and devoured half of it in one massive bite. "Which is why I'm coming with you."

"No, you're not."

"Yeah, I am. Stop fighting. It's decided. You might be stubborn, but I'm stubborner."

"That's not a word."

"Sure it is."

"Bris…"

"I won't hold you up at all, if that's what you're worried about. I'm already packed. My bag's in my truck."

She raised an eyebrow. So he'd been planning on not taking no for an answer all this time? He might be easygoing most of the time, but he was right—when he wanted to, he could be just as hard-headed as she was.

She was about to argue some more, just because it was Bris, and they liked sparring and getting each other riled. But then his phone buzzed. He fished it out of his pocket and brought it to his ear.

"Bris." A pause. "Oh. Hey."

His eyes went up and found Rylie's. "Yeah. Yeah. She's right here. No. She hasn't."

Rylie stared at him. From the tone of his voice and the buzz of a severe female voice coming through the receiver, she knew exactly who it was—Kit Brandon, their supervisor.

From the look on Brisbane's face, it was clear something was up.

What is it? she mouthed, as he listened intently.

New case, he mouthed back. *Something in Montana.*

Well, speak of the devil. They'd have to pass right through Elephant Hole to get there.

"Here, Kit, let me put you on speaker."

He set the phone down on the table between them. There was no need to debate it now. They'd both be heading back west to deal with another case. Together.

But she'd have to try to find the time to sneak away and look into Elephant Hole. Preferably by herself.

CHAPTER THREE

Rylie absently took another donut out of the bag, even though she wasn't hungry anymore, and took a bite as she listened to Kit speak.

"There was a body of a hitchhiker found last night," their special agent in charge said, in her usual sensible, unemotional, businesslike voice. "Outside of a town called Bearmouth."

It was vaguely familiar to Rylie, again along the I-86 corridor, but she couldn't quite place it.

"Bearmouth?" Michael asked.

"You know it?" Rylie asked.

"It's east of Missoula," he said with a short nod. Of course, Missoula. His hometown. "Used to go hunting there with my buddies."

She stared at him. Though Michael Brisbane was always talking—he could carry on a conversation with a wall—he never did say much about himself. She'd thought that unlike her, such a happy-go-lucky type like him had had an ideal upbringing. Lately, though, she'd gotten clues that maybe that wasn't the truth; that he was happy despite some childhood trauma, and maybe even put on that smiling façade to hide it. But one thing he always said was that he'd lived in Missoula.

That wasn't where he grew up, though. He'd told her the name of the town in North Dakota where he'd spent his childhood years. Haven. She'd never be able to forget that, because of the way he'd spoken about it. There'd been pain in his eyes. Hurt. *I'm not ever going back to my hometown in North Dakota. I can't.* When she'd asked him why, he'd only replied, *Maybe I'll tell you sometime.*

Now she couldn't help but be curious about it. What had happened to him in Haven? She couldn't help being a little annoyed that though she was usually a closed book, she'd spilled her childhood to him, and while he was usually open and honest about everything, he'd kept the cards of his own traumatic past close to his chest.

"Well, then you know the lay of the land," Kit said. "That's good. And you probably also know it's pretty remote. Other than the interstate running through it, there's not much there until you get to

Missoula. From what I hear, the Highway Patrol in Missoula is the closest police precinct."

"Yeah," Michael said with another nod. "I think there's a gas station and an RV park outside of town there, but not much else. I'm familiar with the Highway Patrol out that way."

This was nothing new. Seemed like most exits in the remote areas of the highway were the same, very bare and empty, with little action. After a while, they all started to run together. And yet… crime found a way, especially on this cursed interstate. She remembered this area because one of the bodies from their recent case had been found there. "So it's near Wineglass?"

"Even farther west of that," Michael explained.

Oh, so definitely closer to Missoula. She opened her phone to the map and looked it up. That was interesting. Though she'd be passing Story Creek, Wyoming, to get there, she needed to focus on this new case. Maren's case had waited twenty years, and could probably wait a little longer, but with this one, time was of the essence. "You said it was a female hitchhiker?"

"That's right. We're still waiting for ID on the body. But another hitchhiker, a Lottie Jones, forty, was walking in the area and stumbled upon it last night."

"Signs of foul play?" Michael asked.

"Most definitely. Hit on the head, strangled, and dumped there. Seems that it might match up with the case of Gary Blake, another victim, this one a male hitchhiker who was found in the area a few weeks ago, same thing. Ligature strangulation from behind."

"Interesting," Rylie said, taking notes on her phone.

"Wolf, I know you said you were taking a few days for personal reasons. But do you think—"

"Absolutely, I'm on this," she said, sharing a glance with Michael. "My days off can wait. Not a problem."

"Okay, great. I've already been in touch with the Highway Patrol in Missoula. They are working on this and told me they'd be sending over the files. I'll have them forwarded to you the moment they come in."

Michael nodded. "Great. If you speak to them, you can tell them we're on our way."

He ended the call and looked up at Rylie, who stood up, throwing the napkins and powder-covered trash into the garbage.

"Look on the bright side. We're already packed."

She had to laugh at him. "It's only you who can find the bright side in a murder investigation, Bris. Let's go. I'll drive this time."

He raised an eyebrow, and she knew what he was thinking. *You're going to head off in the middle of this investigation and check out Elephant Hole, aren't you?*

Rylie couldn't deny it—the thought hadn't just crossed her mind. It was stuck there in the center of her brain, just like Maren's murder all those years before.

*

The ride out to Bearmouth from Rapid City was a long nine hours. For Rylie, it was a long nine hours of thinking about Maren, while trying to keep up with Michael's rambling. Michael had a way of opening his mouth and never shutting it, speaking stream-of-consciousness about anything and everything that popped into his head.

She wished it would drown out the voice in her head. It sounded like Maren, calling to her, begging for her to look into this newest lead. No such luck.

"... And it's funny, because that's what I said. If a tree falls in the woods, the question is not whether it makes a sound. The question is who cares in the first place. Am I right?"

"Mmm-hmm," she said, staring out the window at the endless, rolling yellow hills. The sky was full of heavy dark clouds, threatening rain, but it was unusually warm and sticky.

"And that's the thing about zombies. They come back. Vampires come back, too. Then it got me wondering, if a vampire bites a zombie, does the zombie become a vampire or the vampire become a zombie?"

"Yeah, right," she mumbled, nodding as if she was following him perfectly. In reality, she'd lost him somewhere near the Wyoming border. But he didn't care. He just went on and on, undaunted.

"And that's another thing about the weather. I don't fault the weathermen for being wrong practically all the time. I get it. It's hard. But seriously... you have to wonder. When does it stop being partly sunny and become partly cloudy? Is it, like, a fifty-percent thing? Or some kind of mathematical equation? These are the things that keep me up at night," he said, tapping his fingers on his thighs.

Rylie hit the blinker to go into the left lane and pass another car. She was pushing ninety, but she needed to get there. That was another reason she'd wanted to drive—Brisbane always drove just under the speed limit, like a good Boy Scout. She was always rocking back and forth in the front passenger seat of his truck, wishing he'd go faster.

But even at ninety, she felt like she was going too slow. Like things were passing her by. She'd been antsy when they'd passed the exit for Story Creek, with the brown sign indicating ELEPHANT HOLE STATE HISTORICAL MONUMENT. Now she couldn't fight the feeling like she'd left something behind. Like she wasn't where she needed to be.

Chill out, Rylie. You can look into it later. Maybe on the way back. As soon as you finish with this case.

Unfortunately, there was no telling how long this case would last.

"Dinnertime," Michael said, checking his watch as they passed a sign that announced a steakhouse at the next exit. "That place serves good grub. Want to stop for—"

"I think we should stop in at the Missoula Highway Patrol and see what they know first," she said. "It's pretty urgent."

His face fell. "How did I know you'd say that?"

"Um, because we just had like a half a dozen donuts before we left Rapid City. I'm not even close to being hungry."

"Dude," he said, glaring at her like she was some kind of alien. "That was nine hours ago. You wouldn't even let me go into the convenience store for a Coke when you stopped for gas."

"That's because I really want to get there." She pointed to his phone. The files had come in from Kit hours ago, and though he'd glanced at them, she didn't think he'd given them quite the thorough scrubbing they deserved. "What do the files say?"

He shrugged. "Pretty much what we've been already told. Murdered girl, probably twenties, as of yet unidentified. There was no ID on her."

"And the guy they found last week?"

"His name was Gary Blake. Quiet kid, twenty. From Missoula. His sister said he was on his way east to meet with a boyfriend, someone he'd been talking with online. She was going to drive him, but then her car broke down, so he decided to hitch it there."

"Hmm," she said, making up a list in her mind of people they could talk to. This sister was one. And once they identified the body, there'd be others, of course. "What are the similarities in the cases?"

"The bodies were found in two eastbound locations of I-86. About ten miles apart from each other, set back a little ways from the road. No mention as to whether the murder happened there, or they were murdered elsewhere and dumped. Ligature strangulation, blunt force trauma to the head, but no other signs of bodily trauma, not even defensive wounds." His stomach growled, and he clamped a hand over it. "Calm down, stomach. We know all this already."

"That's it? Nothing else?"

"Yep, that's all they've got."

She let out a little sigh. With that little to go on, this probably wouldn't be an open and shut case.

And that meant Maren would have to wait. But how much longer? It was a case that was twenty years in the making, and she'd already felt that every day, her sister was calling to her, asking for help. She didn't even know what it would feel like, to not have the circumstances of her sister's kidnapping in the back of her mind, haunting her. It seemed impossible.

"All right, let's get over to the Highway Patrol and see if some of the officers can't shed some light on it," she said.

CHAPTER FOUR

Michael Brisbane watched out the window as various places he'd grown familiar with came into view. Missoula had been his hometown for many years, and so he felt comfortable here.

But the trip to get here? Hadn't been so comfortable. Rylie was on edge, and whenever she was on edge, he knew he was in for a bumpy ride.

It was fine. By now, he knew Rylie was a bit of a closed book, someone who didn't like to chat and shoot the breeze. He was okay with that. But it sure made for a tense nine hours. He prided himself on being the affable type of guy who could talk to anyone about anything, but she gave him little to work with. Now, even he was running out of material.

"You ever wonder how certain towns get their names? They can't all be named after Indian tribes, right?" he said as they passed a sign announcing that they were within the city limits. "Take Bearmouth. You think someone saw a bear and said, 'Hey, that bear has a big mouth'? And then just decided to put down roots here and called it Bearmouth?"

She shrugged.

"Or like, take anywhere. Where you're from. Seattle. Is that because it's by the sea?"

She tore her eyes from the road and pointed at his phone. "If you care that much, you can look it up on your phone."

Well, thank goodness. He'd begun to think she'd fallen into a trance. She'd been that way, offering little more than a "hmm" or an "uh-huh" whenever he posed a question. Sometimes, he got the feeling she wasn't even listening to him at all.

He shook his head. "More fun to wonder than to know."

"You're a strange man, Michael Brisbane," she said with a shake of the head.

"I've been told that more than once," he said proudly.

"I don't doubt it."

But truthfully, Rylie was the strange one. People usually trusted him, opened up to him, but he'd gotten to the point where he thought Rylie never would. And just when he thought she'd closed up on him for good, she'd surprised him by telling him about how, in a place called Story Creek, her sister had been kidnapped, her mother murdered.

No wonder she didn't trust anyone. A kid didn't have a thing like that happen to them and emerge without scars. He knew that better than anyone.

She hadn't said much about the event, but it was clearly in the back of her mind. He hadn't wanted to push her, and had been worried she'd expect some quid pro quo—*I told you my darkest secret, now you tell me yours!* So he'd flubbed it, and had acted like a bit of a dismissive jerk, now that he thought about it. She'd been offended, clearly expecting him to act more caring and concerned, but the whole thing had opened up his own box of demons, one he'd been trying to keep the lid on for a long time.

If it weren't for that, he'd have listened to anything she wanted to say. Rylie was an interesting person. The less she talked, the more interested in her he became.

And that probably wasn't a good way to feel, considering they were partners. Rylie took her job very seriously. The last thing she would probably ever do would be crossing the line, making their relationship a personal one. He'd do well to remember that.

Sometimes, though, it was hard, especially when she was in a good mood and teasing him. She liked riling him up, just as much as he liked doing the same to her. Even though they seemed like night and day, they were actually perfect complements of one another.

As they drove, he pointed out various points of interest to her. His old apartment building, where he lived with some buddies when first in the FBI. The high school track where he used to run. The gas station he used to stop at every morning to get coffee.

She looked at it all with mild disinterest. "Hmm."

So she was back inside her own head again. Probably thinking about her sister, and when she was going to break from this investigation and look into the new clue. He couldn't blame her. He'd want to do the same thing, if it was someone from his own family.

They pulled up at the police department, a squat brick building right off the interstate. "Do you know anyone here at the PD?" she asked him as they walked inside.

He snorted. "*Do I know anyone?* Seriously, you have to ask me that? Who did you think I was?"

She stared at him as he reached forward to open the door for her. "So that's a yes?"

He was about to answer when voices inside shouted, "Brizzy! You're back!"

She raised an eyebrow. "Brizzy?"

He shrugged and smiled as he stepped inside, giving high fives to all the officers at the front desk. There were Hoskins and Jimenez, Bellamy and Waluski. They were a motley crew—a bunch of men from their late twenties to late forties, each with a bit of a beer belly, but other than that, completely different. Hoskins was short and fat, Bellamy skinny and basketball-player tall, Waluski looked like he was still a teenager, right down to the acne and bed haircut, and Jimenez was the greaser kid who looked like trouble, even in his police uniform.

Some of them came around the counter to hug him like a brother. "Hey, guys," Michael said. "Good to see you. How have things been?"

"Not bad, not bad," Jimenez said, clapping him on the back. "We were wondering when you were going to show your sorry ass back in town. It's been too long."

"You're telling me," he said with a grin. "Missed you guys. Don't know why. But I did."

They all laughed loudly. Bellamy said, "We feel the same about you. You up for a game tonight? We're playing."

He felt a pang of nostalgia for the old days, when they used to play baseball down at the fields by city hall and then go out for beers. He'd been out with his buddies from the FBI since then, but it wasn't the same as these guys. He said, "I'd like to. But you know about the case I'm on, right?"

"Yes, so we've heard," Detective Hoskins, the most senior member of the group, said. "They roped you into the case of that gay hitchhiker, huh?"

He nodded.

"Good luck with that one. There's not much to go on."

"So it seems," Rylie suddenly spoke up. "But we need to do something so it doesn't happen again. Have you put out any notice against hitchhiking in the area?"

They all looked at her. Bellamy's expression said it all: *And who the hell do you think you are, telling us our business?* "Of course. Obviously. First thing we did."

Michael looked over at Rylie. She didn't look hurt over not being introduced. She was back to her no-nonsense, severe, all-business self. Wanting answers, not friends. "Guys, let me introduce my partner, Rylie Wolf. Wolf, this is Jimenez, Hoskins, Bellamy, and Waluski."

She went around shaking hands, and then, as expected, she went right into it. The woman did not know the meaning of the term *soft touch.* "Can we go somewhere and see everything you've got on the case?"

The boys nodded and glanced over at him for direction, a little shell-shocked by her abrupt approach. They'd get used to it. He shrugged. "Yeah, Rylie's right. We shouldn't waste any time."

"Right this way, then," Hoskins said, leading them to a conference room. As they put their things down, Hoskins said, "I'll be right back with the files."

"Thank you," Rylie said in a clipped manner, staring up at the WANTED posters on the wall. She paced the area as if she was counting the moments.

"Hey," he said, not that he thought he could be any help. "You can take it easy. Everything's under control."

She checked her phone. "It'll be under control when we find this killer."

He reached his hands over his head, stretching his back. "I get it. You're excited to solve this case so you can get back to Story Creek. But it's—"

"You're half-right. I'm excited to solve this case. Or at least try. That's all."

"So you're not antsy because you want to check out Elephant Hole?" He gave her a doubtful look.

"It's waited this long. It can wait longer," she said with a shrug as she continued to pace around the table. "So you're clearly the belle of the ball here, huh, *Brizzy*?"

He gazed at her in confusion, until it struck him—she must've meant the warm welcome they gave him. "Yeah, well. These guys. We were on a baseball team together while I was here. I worked a few cases with them, and so yeah. They're buds."

"You didn't mention you had friends here. But I guess you have a lot of friends everywhere." She said it with the slightest bit of distaste in her voice.

"I guess… Something wrong with having friends?"

"No, it's good," she said with a hitch of the shoulder. "I just think it's funny. You can make friends with anyone."

He grinned. "Yeah. Even you. Amazing."

"Well, I wouldn't call us *friends*," she said with a small smile. "I mean, would we really be spending time together if our job wasn't forcing us to?"

"Yeah, you're right. If it weren't for you, instead of being in this hole, I'd be eating a steak—"

Just then, Hoskins walked in with two small files. He set them on the table, eyeing Michael as if he'd just missed something and wanted to be filled in. Michael wiped the stupid grin from his face and said, "Hey, thanks, Hos," leaning over the files and opening the first one up. "What do we got here?"

"Well, I wasn't on duty when the body of that Gary kid was found. But I did speak to his sister. Real sob story there because the kid was kind of awkward and sickly, and his sister was happy because he'd finally come out of his shell. New boyfriend and all. And then he went out to meet him, and this happened." He shook his head. "Damn shame. Poor kid."

Michael looked over Rylie's shoulder as she paged through the photographs of the crime scene. They were pretty grisly. One showed the back of his head, with a bloody dent at the crown, matting down his shaggy hair. "Hit from behind, huh? Same with the other victim?"

"Yeah. Almost exactly the same."

"No defensive wounds. That suggests the killer knocked them out, then strangled them while they were dazed and couldn't fight back," Rylie mused, almost to herself. "From this, it looks like he was struck a couple times."

The men nodded in agreement.

Hoskins said, "Yeah, the only difference with this one, from what we saw at the location, was that we think he died right there. Hit, tried to run off, hit again. There are footprints in the ground that suggest that." He showed them a photograph to confirm it. "No footprints of the assailant, just of ol' Gary. The other one was dumped. The girl. But other than that, it's pretty much the same shit, different day."

Michael watched as Rylie opened the folder for the murdered woman and paged through. "Candy Fronheiser, huh?"

"Yeah. At least that's the name they gave us. We'll know for sure in about thirty minutes. A brother of the victim is en route to the coroner's right now to perform an identification."

Just as Michael had expected, Rylie said, "Oh, good. We'll be there, too, to ask the brother some questions. I think that will be helpful. Would you like to come along, Detective?"

"Uh, yes," he said, giving Michael a curious look.

"Perfect," she said efficiently, grabbing her purse and heading for the door. "Now if you'll just show me to the nearest restroom, I'll be ready to leave in a moment."

Hoskins backed out the door and pointed the way to her. Michael heard her heels clicking efficiently down the hallway, and then the creak of a door before it slammed shut.

The second it did, Hoskins swung his head back around and stared at Michael. "So are you and the hot agent… you know… together?"

Amazing how these guys could make him feel like he was twelve again. It was something about playing baseball together that brought out the kid in them. He shook his head. "Nah. She's just my partner."

His eyes narrowed. He wanted more dirt. "And how's that going?"

Michael shrugged. "Good?"

"Good?"

"She's a good agent. She's tough."

"And that's all?"

Michael knew exactly what he was digging for, so he was more than happy to play dumb and let him guess. "We've only been partners for going on two months, but it's going well."

Hoskins reached under his blazer and scratched his beer belly. "Yeah, but she's hot. Single? And you're still single, right?" When Michael nodded, he said, "So what's the problem?"

Michael was fully ready to play dumb for as long as Hoskins could keep spouting stupid questions, but now he was just getting annoyed. "What do you mean?"

"I mean that when you were here in Missoula, you were always with the hottest girls. Like in this town, there wasn't a single one you didn't get to. Didn't matter who they were. You dated them."

Michael looked away, shrugging, hoping they could move on to talk about something else. Fat chance. When Hoskins found something that interested him, he clamped onto it, never letting go.

Hoskins wasn't lying, though. He'd often turned them down for a boys' night out so that he could take a woman on a date. Not that it did any good. He never found anyone worthy of going on a second date with. Some would say he was picky. Maybe that was true, to a degree.

Whatever it was, it meant he'd spent a lot of wasted nights, trying to find someone who he was now pretty damn sure didn't exist.

"Yeah, okay, she's an attractive woman. But like I said, she's my partner," he said, gathering up the files. "And as you can probably tell…"

He nodded. "All about business? Got it."

Michael nodded, too, hoping that was the end of it.

But then Hoskins said, "But you never know what could happen one of those nights, when you're both stressed out, far away from home—"

"Who's far away from home?" a voice asked from the hallway.

The men whirled together to find Rylie Wolf standing in the doorway, long hair brushed, a fresh coat of lip gloss on. Her eyes went from man to man as they stared at her in stunned silence. How much of that had she heard?

Then Michael said, "He was just saying that it was sad, what happened to that victim Gary, so far away from home."

She nodded in agreement. "Very sad."

Was it his imagination, or did she look rather suspicious? Like she knew exactly what they'd been talking about a minute before. That was one thing about Rylie Wolf. She was intuitive, and not just when it came to murder cases.

Shit. He'd been afraid that meeting these guys would mean they might reveal something about his past that he'd much rather keep buried, especially around Rylie. He needed to be careful.

"Okay. Are you two ready?" she asked, grabbing the files from the table. "Because I am. Let's go."

CHAPTER FIVE

The coroner's office was only a block away from the police department, near the hospital, so they walked it along the shoulder of the main road, which was busy with evening traffic. Rylie was a little annoyed. Hoskins was supposed to be leading the charge, but he kept hanging back with his "bud," Brizzy, mentioning things that had happened in town, clapping him on the back and saying, "What do you think about that, huh?"

Michael, on the other hand, nodded tightly and didn't say much. He seemed uncomfortable, which Rylie found strange. To be uncomfortable in your own hometown, where everyone knew you?

"Bellamy's engaged," Hoskins said, once again hanging back and leaving her to lead the way, even though she had no idea where to go. There was a sign up ahead that might have said CORONER, so she headed that way. "Can you believe that one?"

"No," Michael said, seeming a little more alive. "Never thought he'd settle down. Who's the lucky lady?"

"Kathy. Kathy Shanks. Remember her?"

"From the Rusty Nail? No kidding."

Hoskins now stood between them, so they'd formed a bit of a line. She heard him say, "Yeah. You dated her once, am I right?"

Her ears perked up. She wasn't sure why; she knew Michael probably had his share of dates, considering he was so charming and handsome. But he was usually so tight-lipped about a lot of things in his past. She had to wonder what kind of girls he was interested in, and why after all this time, he hadn't settled down. Fear of commitment, likely.

But Michael climbed back into his shell and said, simply, "Yeah. Long time ago. But that's really great. She's a nice girl."

A nice girl. But not nice enough for him to marry himself? Definite fear of commitment.

Rylie had just made that decision as Hoskins swerved off toward a parking lot, and she noticed the small white building near the hospital, with a sign on the door that said *Missoula County Medical Examiner and Coroner's Office.*

When they arrived, the coroner was standing out front, near the receptionist. Hoskins made the introductions. "Dr. Morrison, these are Michael Brisbane and Rylie Wolf, of the FBI."

The medical examiner, completely bald and with severe, hooded dark eyes, shook their hands and said, "Well, you might as well come on back with me. I was waiting for the brother of Candy Fronheiser, but he's been delayed." He looked at the young receptionist. "Marie, when he arrives, can you buzz me?"

"Yes, sir," she said.

"I haven't performed the autopsy yet, as I'm still waiting on the ID. But I can make a few assumptions." He led them back through a series of white double doors to the morgue, where a slight body was lying upon one of three metal tables in the center of the room, covered with a white sheet. Even so, white-blonde hair spilled out from under the sheet.

They gathered around it, donning latex gloves, and he pulled back the sheet. Despite the bloodied wound on the top of her head, and the ligature marks around her throat, it was clear she'd once been a very pretty girl. Her skin was the pale green of death, but the body was in remarkably good condition. Rylie leaned forward. "How long has she been dead?"

"Few days. It's been cold, which kept the body pretty well."

"Can you tell the cause of death?" Michael asked.

"The injury to the top of the head started the job. Blunt instrument, obviously," he said, tilting the head slightly to give them a better look. "The strangulation finished the job."

"This similar to the other homicide?" Rylie asked. "You think it could've been the same instrument?"

"Yes. Just from eyeballing it, there's a good chance."

"So a blunt instrument," Michael theorized, crouching to get a better look. "What are we talking about here, Doc? Like a baseball bat?"

"Not that big. Something smaller."

Rylie said, "So, like a hammer of some kind?"

"More like a club," the coroner said.

Michael nodded, lowering the sheet some more so he could have a look at the girl's hands. "No sign of any defensive injuries, then, huh?"

"No. She didn't know what hit her."

There was a buzzing sound overhead, and a voice said, "Dr. Morrison? Victor Fronheiser is here."

The coroner nodded. "I'll be right out." He snapped off his gloves and added, "It's the brother. He came in from Helena. I'll be right back." He went to the door, leaving the three of them alone.

Hoskins shook his head in dismay. "Shame. Pretty girl. Looks so young."

Rylie had to agree, as she pulled the sheet back over the woman. A girl that young, she had to wonder if it had been drilled into her head enough that I-86 wasn't the kind of road to hitchhike on. Most people who lived on or near the highway knew that. But if this girl was from Helena, which wasn't on I-86, maybe she hadn't been aware. And now it was too late.

The door swung open, and a young man in a plaid shirt and jeans, with shaggy hair that hung over his collar, stepped in. He was holding a cowboy hat and wearing boots, a real cowboy, if ever she'd seen one.

The poor man looked absolutely shell-shocked as the coroner pulled the sheet back. He hung his head, squeezed his eyes closed, and began to sob quietly. "That's her. Who could've done such a thing to my little sis? Oh, god!"

Brisbane approached the man cautiously. "I understand this has to be hard for you. I'm Agent Brisbane, and this is Agent Wolf, of the FBI," he said in a gentle voice as the man stood there, staring at the sheet-covered body. "We'd like to ask you questions, if you're feeling up to it."

Victor fixed his gaze on the agent. He'd gone right past the grief stage into anger. "Absolutely. If it'll help us catch the bastard that did this, you can question me as long as you like."

Rylie said, "Why don't we step outside into the waiting area, where it's a little more comfortable?"

They followed her to the lobby, where there were a few rows of seats like at the DMV, except that they were all empty. Propped up in the corner of the room was a television with a news anchor, droning on about the events of the day. Michael wasted no time in finding the remote and turning it off. Rylie spotted a small beverage service in the corner with carafes of coffee and a water cooler. "Can I get you something to drink? Coffee? Water?"

He swallowed. "Water. Please."

Before she could, Brisbane was already on it. He handed the man a paper cup full of water and they sat down together. The man sipped it, his hands shaking. "Did they—do they have any idea of who could've done this to her?"

"We don't know yet, but we're going to find out for you," Brisbane said. "When was the last time you saw Candy?"

Victor drained the cup and crumpled it in his fist. "A few days ago. Monday, I guess. She'd been planning this road trip for the better part of the year. She was so excited to head out."

"So this was a planned trip," Rylie mused aloud. Interesting, considering that if that was the case, she should've had a backpack or luggage with her. And the notes never mentioned anything like that. She made a mental note of it and said, "Where was she headed? Do you know?"

"She was going to go off through Washington State, head south, and eventually land in L.A." He smiled sadly. "She was my little sister. Five years my junior, and most brothers and sisters with that kind of gap don't see eye to eye, but she was the light of my life. Always laughing and smiling and putting people in a good mood. I can't believe she's gone."

"Do you know anything about why she might've been out there on the highway?"

"Yeah." He laughed sadly. "She hated Helena. Couldn't wait to get out and make a name for herself. She just graduated from the University of Montana with an acting degree, so she was going off the way most drama majors go—to Hollywood. But with her—we all knew she would make it. Not only was she beautiful, she had talent, too. Grit."

"And she told you of her plans to… what? Hitch her way there?" Brisbane asked.

Victor shook his head. "No, god no. She told me she wasn't hitching. If she had, I would've told her that was dangerous and locked her up in her room, thrown away the key. She was always taking risks like that, accepting rides with guys she didn't know. 'He's harmless,' she'd say to me. I told her you never knew, but she kept insisting she'd be fine. So I guess I should've known. That's probably why she told me she and a group of friends were heading out by van, on a road trip. She knew I would've tried to talk her out of hitching it there."

"I see. And you said she was planning on going with some friends? Do you know their names?"

He shook his head. "She didn't tell me. If she was going with someone, it could've been anyone in town—she had so many friends. I don't think any of them could've done something like this. I mean, she had a lot of friends, but she loved everyone. She didn't have enemies."

Rylie was about to ask another question, when the man pounded his thighs with both fists.

"Now that I think about it, she *was* going alone. She was fearless like that. Independent. I always told her it was going to get her in trouble. Candy was really pretty. She attracted creeps. But the thing was, she was nice to all of them. Too nice. I should've stopped her. I should've known. If only she hadn't hidden it from me," he said, shaking his head in sorrow.

Michael put a hand on the man's shoulder. "Hey. You couldn't have known this. Plenty of people hitch their way across the country and nothing like this ever happens. She just met up with the wrong person."

"I guess. I just can't believe she's gone," he said again. Then he snapped his head up. "What about you guys? You have any clues? Any signs pointing to who might've done this to her?'

Rylie nodded. "There is another similar case, from last week. There was a man who was killed in a similar fashion and left along the highway, close to where your sister was found. Do you happen to know a Gary Blake, from Missoula?"

Victor shook his head. "No… he was killed, too? In the same way? So what are we dealing with, some kind of serial killer?"

Brisbane nodded. "It's too early to tell at this point. It could just be a coincidence. But it means there's a good chance that whoever killed your sister selected her at random. That it was just a crime of opportunity, and she was there when he was looking for a victim. Either way, we plan to get to the bottom of it." He handed the man his business card. "In case you think of anything else that could be helpful."

Victor stood up. "Thanks. Thank you. I appreciate it. You'll let me know if you make any progress?"

"Of course," Rylie said. "We have your information."

They watched him through the windows as he went outside, stepped into his pickup, and drove off. When his truck was gone, Michael said, "It's looking more and more like the murders of Gary Blake and Candy Fronheiser are related, huh?"

"Yeah. It does seem that way."

"So we might just have ourselves another serial killer," he said. "Where to next, Boss?"

Rylie looked over at Hoskins, who'd been standing against a wall across the room, watching them work. "Would you be able to get me a list of Gary Blake's relatives in the area? You said he lived in Missoula, right?"

"He does. But he doesn't have many relatives. Just a sister, Sarah Blake. She lives in an apartment complex about a mile from here."

Brisbane spoke up. "And what about that hitchhiker? The one who found the second victim's body? Is she still around?"

Hoskins nodded. "She is. We put her up in the Best Western across the street. She didn't have anywhere to stay. I think her plans were to continue east, but she might be rethinking that, considering what happened."

"All right," Rylie said. "Let's flip a coin for where to start first and see if we can't shed more light on this killer."

CHAPTER SIX

Rylie led the charge this time, as they walked across the street to the three-story brick hotel with the giant statue of a cowboy in the front of it. It wasn't the lap of luxury, but it was a well-maintained property, with a lobby full of modern furniture and fixtures. They even had free cookies at reception, for guests.

Of course, that's just what Michael Brisbane dug into, the second they stepped up to the desk. He grabbed one, then three more, furtively looking around like a child as they waited for the front desk clerk to arrive. He shoved them into the pockets of his blazer, just as a sickly-thin kid with a buzz cut peered through the door behind the desk, sucking on a juice box.

"Sorry. Er, sorry," he said, nearly choking on his juice. "Didn't hear you come in."

Contrary to what Rylie had said, they hadn't flipped a coin. Based on what Hoskins had said, the woman who'd found the second victim, Lottie Jones, sounded like she was more likely to pull up stakes and set off, so Rylie made the decision that they should head over to the Best Western and talk to her first. Hoskins was called back to headquarters on another job, leaving Rylie and Michael to handle the questioning themselves.

"It's okay, buddy," Michael said, still chewing. "We're looking for someone who's staying with you. A Lottie Jones? Can you ask her to come out here?"

He went to his computer and tapped something in. "Yeah, she's—" He stopped when he noticed something on Brisbane's shirt. Crumbs. "Wait. Those are for guests. Who are you, anyway?"

"Sorry," Brisbane said, reaching into his pocket and pulling out his credentials, which he flashed to the kid.

The clerk's eyes widened. "Real FBI, huh? What's the FBI doing out here? Does it have to do with the murder?"

"What do you know about a murder?" Rylie asked.

He shrugged. "Not much. Just that it was in the paper. A dead body found by the interstate. Is that true?"

Michael nodded. "Unfortunately. Good reminder to be safe. Can you get us Lottie Jones, buddy?"

"Oh. Right." He tapped into his computer again and picked up his phone.

As they waited, they paced the floor, Rylie stopping in front of a giant art map of the state of Montana. She found the star that indicated their location and followed it back along I-86 to Story Creek RV park, and Elephant Hole. The places themselves were too small to be listed on the map, but it didn't matter. Rylie had looked at maps of it so many times, she knew it by heart.

The distant ding of an elevator snapped her from her thoughts, and a moment later, a slim woman in a denim skirt, tank top, and cowboy boots appeared in the hall. Her face was weathered and creased, her eye makeup running and flaking. She looked tired, and had an old, frayed backpack over her shoulder. "You're the FBI?" she asked, running an eye over each of them.

Rylie came forward first. "Yes, are you Lottie Jones?"

She nodded.

"This is Agent Wolf," Brisbane said, showing her credentials. "And I'm Michael Brisbane. Can we sit and talk for a little about what you saw?"

They guided her over to a table in the breakfast area and sat down. Michael said, "Can I get you coffee before we start?"

She shook her head and checked her phone. "We might have to cut this short. My boyfriend George is coming to pick me up when he gets off work."

"No problem," Rylie said. "So where were you headed last night, that you were alone on the interstate?"

She fastened Rylie with a hard stare, then rolled her eyes. "Okay, okay, I was hitchhiking. But I didn't have nowhere to go. My boyfriend and I had had a fight and I was trying to get away from him. Didn't get far."

"Where were you attempting to go?"

She shrugged. "Anywhere? In my head, I had an idea of making it all the way to Indiana. But I only made it a few miles. My boyfriend has a place in an RV park south of here, and I was living with him."

"And so what time did you head out last night?"

She tapped her fingernails, coated with chipped red paint, nervously on the table. "It was late. After midnight. That's when I'd gotten off my shift and headed home. When I got there, well, George had *company*, if you know what I mean. Needless to say, I didn't stick around." She rolled her eyes. "I just grabbed whatever I could and took off."

Michael raised an eyebrow. "So… you're going back to George, then? After what he did? That's rough. I'm sorry that happened to you."

She started to nod, but Rylie looked over at him. Who cared about her love life? Someone was dead. Sometimes, Michael got too concerned with the lives of the people affected by the murders, instead of focusing on the murders themselves. "And how did you manage to find the body?"

"I was just walking down the road, trying to mind my own business, and—"

"But you were hitchhiking. So you were trying to find a ride?" Rylie corrected.

She sighed. "Yes, okay, I was. I remember a guy in a blue or black sportscar came, and I was going to catch a ride with him. But he wound up being such a creep, so I told him no thanks. I might have been desperate but I wasn't in the mood for risking my life."

"Did he threaten you?"

"No. I just got the feeling I'd be fending off his advances and roving hands all night long, if you know what I mean. I'd rather freeze to death on the side of the road. So I told him to buzz off."

"You have any information on the creep? What he looked like—"

"I couldn't see him very well. He just had thick hands. A deep voice. And I think, from his shadow, thick, curly hair. But that's all I know."

Rylie made a note of this. It was something worth looking into. "So you told the driver 'no thanks' on the ride, and then what happened?"

"I realized I had to pee. So I went a little off the road, did my business, and when I was coming back, that's when I noticed her. I noticed the hair. It was so blonde, it glowed in the moonlight. At first, I thought it was a dead animal, but then I noticed hands and legs and realized it was a girl. She was just dumped there, like trash." She blew out a breath. "Poor thing. I'll never forget that for as long as I live."

"You say she was dumped there. So you don't think that she was killed there?"

Lottie shrugged. "I don't know. What do I know? It just looked like a place you'd dump a body." She shivered. "And so I called George, who sent out the police. They put me up here for the night."

"And now you're headed back to the RV park," Michael mused.

"Yeah, well. George and I had a talk and made up," she said, not sounding too thrilled with the prospect. Then she leaned forward. "But if I'm being honest with you, I don't want to go out on that cursed road ever again. Not after what I've seen."

Rylie nodded. She couldn't blame her.

Just then, there came the sound of a blaring horn, incessant and annoyed. Michael stood up and peered out the window. "If your guy George drives an F-150, he's here for you, Lottie."

She nodded and popped up, rolling her eyes. "He's so impatient. Do you have any other questions?"

Michael handed her his card. "No, but if you need anything, just give us a call." He patted her upper arm. "You take care of yourself, Lottie."

She beamed at him, flattered. "Thank you."

Rylie groaned inwardly. He had that effect on women. Obviously. He was so nice and concerned with them. He didn't just barrel through with questions, no-nonsense, like she did. He had the softest touch sometimes.

They watched her go, and it looked like the moment Lottie got into the car, they began arguing, gesturing wildly at one another, faces tight.

Michael shook his head. "Poor woman. She has nowhere else to go."

She gazed at him. "Yeah. Can we get back to the case?"

His eyes shifted away from the road to her. "You don't care?"

"I do care. About finding the killer."

"There's more to this job than just finding killers," he pointed out.

"But the most important part is finding the killer," she said, heading out the double doors.

He followed closely. "Maybe, but it doesn't hurt to be nice to people. We've been over this. You have to be human, too."

"That's why I have you. You can be human. Be my public relations team. And I'll do the hard stuff and find the killer. Okay?"

He didn't say anything to her as they walked along the road, back to the police department. She looked over at him. He was chewing on one of the cookies he'd stolen from the hotel. "So where to next?" he finally said. "To talk to Gary Blake's sister?"

She nodded. "Don't you think so?"

He smirked. "Does it matter? You're the lead on this. I'm just the PR team, apparently."

*

Sarah Blake, Gary Blake's sister, lived in the Covered Bridge apartments, only a few blocks away from the main area. The complex was a vast configuration of several buildings arranged to form a middle courtyard. All of them looked the same, with dark shingles and small windows. After walking back and forth through the buildings, they finally found J1, which was the Blake residence.

Rylie knocked on a chipped, mustard-collared door. She looked back at Michael, who'd been pretty silent on the ride over. "Don't tell me you're angry at me for calling you PR?"

He shook his head. "I'm not."

Maybe he wasn't. Michael didn't exactly get angry. But she got the feeling there was something there, something more like... disappointment. Like he wanted her to be a mother hen, to care about these people. She did, really; even though she dealt with victims of loss every day, she wasn't completely heartless. She'd been through it herself. But after bottling those feelings inside for so long, lending sympathy to people experiencing a similar grief only made her own hurt threaten to leak out.

Not to mention that she also had it in her mind that the sooner they got this done with, the quicker she could get back to Elephant Hole. So all she wanted to do was cut to the chase.

But Michael was right. Maybe she was coming off as a little cruel and overly focused when it came to the police work. Even if it wasn't her strong point, maybe she could stand to show a little more compassion. She'd just have to block out her own hurt.

She vowed to try harder from now on, as the door opened, revealing a startlingly pretty woman. The only flaw in her skin seemed to be around her pale-blue eyes, which looked red and rimmed in dark circles from crying. Though she didn't appear to be wearing makeup and her blonde hair was thrown in a messy bun at the top of her head, she was model-beautiful. The giant cardigan she was wearing did little to hide her statuesque, perfectly proportioned body.

Rylie expected Michael to take the lead and say something, as he usually did, so at first, she said nothing. When he didn't speak, she looked over at him. He seemed frozen in awe.

"Uh, hello," the woman said, looking at each of them in turn as she pulled her cardigan closed. "Are you the police?"

Rylie finally pulled out her credentials. "Sarah Blake? I'm Agent Rylie Wolf and this is Agent Michael Brisbane, of the FBI."

"Hi. Do you have news about Gary?"

Rylie shook her head. "Just wanted to ask some routine questions."

"Oh, all right," she said with a sigh. "Come in. I've answered a million questions for the police, but I'm sure you have more."

She stepped inside to an apartment so full of paintings and photographs that the color of the walls was a mystery. There were artsy dance posters all over the wall, too, women doing grand jetes and standing in front of barres. There was only one room, which contained a kitchenette along with a small sofa and a beanbag chair situated around a glass coffee table.

Rylie took a seat on the sofa, sinking into the cushion so far, she wondered if she'd ever get out. No room for Michael. She figured he'd see that, and her predicament, as she shifted to pull herself out of the abyss, when without notice, he moved to the side of the couch and lowered himself in, saying, "So you're a dancer, huh?"

He didn't even seem to notice that they were now both sinking into the center of the sofa, their thighs pressed uncomfortably together.

"Yeah, I was in the Tucson Ballet for a few years, but then I retired to come up here and start my own studio," she said dismissively. "My therapist says I should keep busy. Try to forget. But I might as well talk about him, because there's no way I'm going to be able to forget. Not my little brother."

"You were close, huh?" Michael said, oblivious to the fact that they were sinking even closer together.

Probably not as close as we are right now, Rylie thought, putting her hand on the armrest and yanking herself out of the confines of the demon sofa. He didn't seem to notice this at all.

Sarah sat on the edge of the beanbag chair, her tiny body barely making a dent in it. "Yes, he was my baby brother. Such a good kid."

"I'm so sorry for your loss," Michael said, looking around the place. "He lived here with you?"

She nodded. "Ever since my parents died. I came back here from Arizona when they did, to finish raising him."

Michael just gazed at her in wonder. "So you're alone now."

She nodded.

"Well, let me ask a question," Rylie said, since it was clear Michael wasn't going to get to the heart of the matter. How did he expect her to have compassion when all he did was pussy-foot around the subject? "Did you know he was leaving?"

"Yeah. He was a quiet kid, and I was really worrying about him." She piled her hands in her lap and stared at them. "He was really smart. Graduated from college when he was only nineteen. After college, he moved back with me and wasn't sure what he wanted to do with his life. I told him he could stay with me as long as he liked. I knew he was gay, and being from such a small town, he had a hard time meeting people like him. He told me he was chatting online with a guy who lived in Minneapolis. He thought he was in love and wanted to meet up with him. I was having car trouble, or else I would've taken him. I told him he should fly but he didn't have the money and wanted to hitch a ride out there. So he did."

That meant that where Candy was headed west, Gary was headed east. So if this was a serial killer, the direction where they were headed, didn't seem to matter.

"Do you know the name of the man he was going to meet?" Rylie asked.

"Yeah. It was Rory. Rory Chambers." She stood up. "I gave the police all of his information, Gary's computer, all these text messages they had going back and forth. As far as I know, Rory's beside himself. He feels like this is all his fault."

"You ever meet him?" Michael asked.

"No. I talked to him on the phone, though." She smiled sadly. "I know what you're thinking—that maybe Gary got involved with the wrong guy, someone who was catfishing him. The police thought that, too. But Rory was the real deal. They used to chat online all the time."

Rylie's lips twisted. That didn't mean he was real. She'd investigated enough crimes that started out with online dating to know that those doing the deceiving could be awfully slick, going through all sorts of ruses to appear like real people. It was worth checking deeper into this Rory Chambers's file to find out more.

"When was the last time you spoke to your brother?"

"Before he left, the day he disappeared. He was going to call me when he reached the border of Montana, but never did. That's when I called the police to report him missing," she explained, her brow knitting. "And then a day after that, I learned they'd found his body. He never got very far. They found his body in Drummond, I think. So that meant he was killed just after he left."

She buried her face in her hands.

Michael scrambled to rise and rushed to her, consoling her. She sobbed quietly. "Why would anyone do anything like that to him? He wasn't hurting anyone! He was such a nice, quiet soul, not a mean bone in his whole body."

Michael rubbed her back gently. "It's okay. It's going to be all right."

While he did this, Rylie paced the small apartment. It didn't seem there was much more to get from this than was already in the file. Rory Chambers seemed like a good possibility, but was probably too obvious. If he'd been in the area from Minneapolis, the police would've pegged him as a suspect. But despite that possibility, there was nothing in the file to say that, which meant that they'd likely already cleared him.

"Do you know of anyone that your brother might have had troubles with? Someone who wanted to hurt him?"

Sarah looked up, her face full of fresh tears. "No, no one. He was such a good kid. Everyone liked him."

That's what she'd said before. And while there was the possibility of it being a hate crime, if this was somehow related to Candy Fronheiser's murder, then that probably wasn't true.

"All right. Thanks for your time." She went to the door.

When she turned around, Michael was still stroking the woman's back. She rolled her eyes and cleared her throat.

He popped up. "Right." He took the business card out of his wallet and handed it to the distraught woman. "Please call me."

Rylie stared at him, eyes narrowed, waiting for the rest of the script: *If you think of anything else.* But it seemed to have slipped his mind.

She opened the door and stepped out. Michael lingered there, like a little boy who wanted to ask for a Popsicle. Finally, Rylie had to reach over and physically yank him out of the woman's doorway.

When the door closed, she muttered, "Really smooth."

"Huh?"

She walked faster. "Nothing."

"That woman was… wow. Gorgeous." He still seemed shocked.

"Uh-huh. You think you might want to get ahold of your teenage hormones in order to remember we're working on a case?" She stampeded ahead, toward the parking lot.

He easily caught up with her. "What do you mean?"

“I mean… and I quote… ‘*Please call me*.’” She mimicked his voice, all breathy and lovesick. It really didn’t sound much like he had, but she didn’t care.

He frowned. “You know what I meant. I meant if she thought of anything else. I didn’t think I had to say it all.”

“Yeah. Right. That was just a tad too obvious,” she muttered, grabbing her keys from her purse. “Are you going to be okay?”

As he opened the door and climbed inside the car, he didn’t say anything. He stared at his lap as she started the car and began to pull out of the parking space. Then he said, “I’m sorry. I’m shit when it comes to beautiful women.”

She stared at him, hardly knowing what to feel. She was fine if that meant his not stumbling over himself when he first met her meant that she was not among the beautiful—she knew that already. But it was such a funny thing for him to admit. Here he was, charming to almost everyone, and he couldn’t put two words together in front of someone who was just as beautiful as he was?

She just laughed. “I’ll say. But luckily, you won’t have to talk to her again, regarding the case. I don’t think she’ll help much. But maybe she will *just call you* for another reason?”

He brought his eyes up to meet hers, then shook his head and rubbed the side of his face. “Eh, nah. I don’t want to date anyone.”

“Why not?” she blurted. The second it was out, she felt silly. Who cared? “I mean, she seems nice. And you’re attracted to her.”

He shrugged. “I don’t need to complicate my life any further, I think.”

He was probably referring to the long-distance relationship thing, since he lived in Rapid City now. But as much as she wanted to ask, she bit her tongue. She’d spent too long on this subject, so long, one would probably think she *cared*. And she definitely didn’t want anyone to think that. *Time to make light of things.* She said, “I’m surprised you didn’t already date her, considering how your buddies said you’d dated every girl in Missoula.”

He chuckled, mostly to himself. “Yeah. Must’ve missed her.” She was about to ask him more about it, that curiosity about him welling inside her, but he shrugged. “So with that, I think we’re at a dead end, huh?”

Back to the case. That was where they needed to be. Who cared about his love life? She wasn’t sure why she’d let that distract her. Not when she had to get things moving so she could go back east.

Rylie pulled out of the parking lot, heading to the police department. "Yeah. I mean, the killer could be anyone. I get the feeling it's random, considering the victims don't have much in common. They are different people, going different places. The only thing that links them is that they were hitchhikers. So the killer acts whenever he has the opportunity to pick someone—anyone—up."

"Yeah." He sighed and looked out the window. "Let's go back to headquarters and check out those files again. See if there's anything we missed."

"You read my mind," Rylie said, hoping he couldn't read *everything* in there. Because if he could, then he'd probably see that, as much as she didn't want to be, she was a tiny bit jealous of Sarah Blake for having captured Michael Brisbane's attention like that.

CHAPTER SEVEN

Bill Matthews was out for blood.

He sat at his desk in the FBI's Field Office for the Analysis of Violent Crime in Seattle, stewing. He had been Rylie Wolf's supervisor before she went east to Rapid City. At the time, he'd been thrilled to let her go—in fact, he'd made it happen—because she was a thorn in his side. She was the one constantly belittling him in front of the others, questioning his authority, making him feel like the laughingstock of the department. She was the one who showed him no respect whatsoever. She was the one who always had some snide comment whenever he gave a directive. He'd thought it would mean he'd never have to hear from the woman again.

But he'd been dead wrong.

Instead, all he'd done, since shipping her off two months ago, was hear of a string of successful cases out of her beat, on that Highway Thru Hell, I-86.

And he'd had enough.

"Rich!" he shouted as he saw the man pass his office door.

Cooper Rich reversed direction and appeared in the doorway. "Yeah?" he said. Was he imagining it, or was the junior agent getting annoyed with him? *He better watch it. I can make him or break him. Just like I did with Wolf.*

Or at least, he'd *tried* to do that with Rylie. He hadn't necessarily been successful. And that was the whole damn point.

"Come in. Close the door."

He stepped in and did as he was told. He sat down, eyes already rolling back to the ceiling, sighing deeply. "Let me guess. Rylie Wolf?"

Matthews nodded. Every time he'd called Rich in, lately, Rylie Wolf was behind it. "I need you to do some legwork for me."

Rich pressed his lips together, as if he was fighting not to say something he knew could get him in trouble. Finally, he blurted, "We've been over this. She's not your concern anymore. You haven't been able to stick anything to her on these cases, so maybe you should just move on and—"

"Forget about it?" Matthews frowned. Like he could possibly do that. The woman had weaseled her way into his brain somehow, and he couldn't seem to pry her out. "Bullshit. She's made a load of mistakes, leaving everyone else to pay for them. On behalf of those people she's screwed over, it's my duty to see this through."

Rich shook his head. "Look. We've been over this. Do you have anything else on the Moses Bedelbaum issue?"

Matthews grinned. His only saving grace had been a complaint of unlawful search, made by a man named Moses Bedelbaum. He'd been big in the drug and sex slave trade, a real scumbag. Put in jail by the Golden Girl herself. Bedelbaum had complained about it, and it would've gone absolutely nowhere, if not for Matthews picking it up and running with it. It was his chance.

And he was going to run it as far as he had to, in order to see Rylie Wolf go down.

He held up a sheet of paper. "Yep. I have to say, I'm compiling a pretty big file where the Bedelbaum issue is concerned. I've collected a few more statements on record from criminals put in prison by Rylie Wolf, who are outraged over her unorthodox practices. It doesn't look very good for her. So if there's something you want to add…"

Rich shook his head as he sifted through the pile. "Some of these criminals are the worst of the worst. Who cares if they were manhandled? Rylie Wolf's half the size of some of these guys. This is all B.S. and you know it. I told you. I don't want to be involved, and I sure as hell am not going to be forced into giving a statement that she harassed some criminals. She's a damn good agent."

Matthews sat back, shaking his head slowly. Matthews had hoped that he'd be able to turn Rylie's one good friend in the Seattle field office against her. That would've been nice, to have him testify what a loose cannon she was. If he couldn't do that, the least Rich could've done was tell her she was in danger, force her to keep a low profile and stay out of the headlines. But he wasn't even sure Rich had done that. He was loyal, that was for sure.

Loyal to Rylie Wolf.

Which meant he was just another thorn in Matthews's side. Matthews would have to consider transferring him somewhere else, too.

"Get out of here," he mumbled dismissively, shooing him away with both hands.

"With pleasure," Rich said, jumping up and heading out.

Matthews scowled after him, then looked at the piles of complaints he'd amassed over Rylie Wolf. He'd get her eventually. That was inevitable.

Suddenly, an idea sprang into his head. "Wait."

Rich froze and rolled his eyes to the ceiling again. He spun. "Yes?"

Matthews smiled. "You just finished that double homicide, didn't you?"

"Yes…" Rich said cautiously. He was clearly already on to him. Good.

"I think I have a job for you." He stacked the papers together on the table. "These complaints need investigating. I think it would be a good idea to have someone close to the case reporting on it, letting me know exactly what's going on."

His mouth hung open a full five seconds before he began to speak. "You want me to go and spy on Wolf?"

He nodded. "I think it's prudent, considering the allegations against her. We can't have someone who's unfit on our force, can we?"

It wasn't just prudent. It was perfect.

Cooper Rich shook his head slightly. "Hell no. I'm not going to spy on her."

He grinned. "Sure you are. It's a direct order." *And you're a military man. You never go against a direct order from a superior.*

Cooper hesitated. "She'll be on to me. She's not an idiot. Me going out there out of nowhere? She'll suspect something."

The more Rich dragged his feet, the more Bill Matthews wanted to reach behind his own back and give it a pat. "Eh, don't worry about it. I'll manufacture some excuse for you to be out there. She won't suspect a thing."

And even if she did, good. She'd know to watch herself.

Rich still wavered. What the hell? Why was he acting like he'd just sentenced him to die by firing squad? "Why me, though? I'm her friend. I could tell you that she's up to nothing bad and—"

"Would you do that? Would you lie? I don't think so, Rich. You're a good agent. Straight as an arrow. You report things as you see them."

He fisted his hands. "And I already reported to you that she did nothing wrong."

"But you were never her partner. You weren't close enough. Maybe, if you get a little closer, if you observe her, you'll see something. She's in Montana, by the way. Just arrived there on a new case."

His face fell into a deep scowl. That was Cooper Rich. A sterling member of the team. Unlike his good friend, he never did anything that went against orders from a higher-up. And if it turned out that Cooper Rich failed him on this? If he lied? Well, all the more reason to ax him from the force.

As far as Matthews could see, it was win-win. Still, he needed to sweeten the deal.

"If you do a good job with this, Rich? That promotion you've been eyeing is as good as yours."

Cooper Rich's eyes widened. His fists clenched tighter. "You serious?"

"Dead."

Without a word, Cooper Rich turned and walked to the door, his head down, his fists still clenched tight.

"Rich, I'll take that as a yes! Pack up. I expect you on the next flight out to Missoula," he said, smiling to himself.

"Yes, sir," Rich mumbled.

CHAPTER EIGHT

It was after eight in the evening by the time Rylie and Michael returned to the Missoula police department. Rylie fixed them two strong cups of coffee, and she and Michael sat down in the conference room to scour the files of the two victims, looking for clues.

Rylie stared across the table, trying to make sense of everything she'd learned. That is, until she noticed Michael had turned his blazer pockets inside out and was picking something from the lining, putting it into his mouth. "What are you doing?"

He shrugged. "Cookie crumbs."

She curled her lip. "Ew."

"What do you want me to do? There's no damn vending machine in this building." He picked another crumb out and sucked it off his fingers. "I'm wasting away, thanks to you. What do you run on, the misery of those around you?"

"Ha, ha." She rolled her eyes and looked at the files. Truthfully, she was getting a little hungry, and there wasn't much to go on. Her eyes were crossing. It was probably a good idea to call it a night and start up again when they had fresh eyes. "Just a few more minutes, and then we can find dinner and a hotel."

"No need on the hotel. My man Hoskins has a big place not far from here. He says we can stay with him."

She wrinkled her nose. Staying in a hotel day in and day out was dreary, but she didn't want to impose on anyone. Plus, that seemed a little too close for comfort with Michael. At least, with the hotel, they usually got their own rooms. "He has two guest rooms?"

Michael tilted back in his chair, grabbed a pen off the table, tossed it up, and caught it. "That's what he said. He's going through a divorce. I think he might be a little lonely over there."

Rylie's nights alone were her time to recharge. To get completely away from her cases. She didn't want to spent that time sharing a bathroom with the other investigators on the case. But she was too tired to complain. "All right. I guess that would be okay."

"Good. He already left for the night but he gave me the address. Said anytime we wanted to stop by, we could," he said, yawning, as she scrutinized the files one last time. "So do you think we should stop, get some pizza or something, and head on over there—"

"I think our best way to attack this is to look into each victim's route. Where they stopped, what they did. Try to piece that together. Maybe they have something in common," she said, shifting the papers.

"Yeah. I was just going to say that," he said, his chair falling back into place. "But how do we do that? You heard Sarah. Gary Blake wasn't even on the road for long. His body was dumped in Drummond, not even fifty miles east of Missoula."

"Right… but he stopped somewhere. Look." She pulled out a bank statement and pushed it over to him. "Gary's wallet was found on him. He last used his debit card at the Gas Express in Clinton, Montana."

He raised an eyebrow. "And Candy? Was she there?"

Rylie pushed more paper around, looking for the answer. "It doesn't say. I don't know if they got that far. And if she was, maybe she used cash. But I think it's worth checking out. She was a pretty girl. Someone might remember her."

He yawned again and stood up, pulling out his phone. "Yeah, I guess we should."

She grabbed her keys. "Who are you calling?"

"My boy Hos," he said, his fingers working. "I'm telling him not to wait up for us and to leave the key in the mailbox. Let's go."

CHAPTER NINE

The town of Clinton was twenty miles east of Missoula on I-86, so by the time they got there, it was almost nine. Rylie had been dragging under the harsh fluorescent lights of the precinct's conference room, but now that she had the coffee flowing through her veins, she felt her second wind coming on.

Michael, however, looked beat. He leaned his head against the window and didn't speak. She thought maybe he was sleeping, but she didn't want to wake him. The quiet was a nice change of pace.

The Gas Express was the only gas station around for miles. Even so, it had several cars parked by the pumps, and a few at a small, nameless diner nearby that only said, "EAT." When they pulled into the parking lot outside the gas station's small convenience store and she cut the engine, Michael's head lolled to face her, and she realized he was asleep.

"We're here," she said gently.

His big blue eyes fluttered open and then closed again. "Just go without me, Mom."

Mom? She stared at him. *Seriously, Mom?* She knew she didn't have all of Sarah's grace and beauty, but she was *his* age. What about her gave him Mom vibes? Was it her voice?

She smacked him and growled, "Wake up, idiot. We're here."

His eyes blinked open, and he rubbed them. "Geez. I was out. I was having the weirdest dream."

"No kidding," she mumbled, wondering if it had to do with him driving around with his mother. She got out of the truck without waiting for him, marching right into the small store.

He followed a few seconds later, still rubbing his eyes. She looked around at the place, which was barely big enough for the cash register, the cigarette case behind the cashier, a rack of chips and candy, and a refrigerated case with drinks. A large, pot-bellied man in a trucker's cap that said ACE was checking out, and she had to press up against his sweaty body as he squeezed his way around her.

Grimacing, she went up to the cashier, a gum-popping girl with part-shaved, part-purple-dyed hair, and presented her badge. “Hi, do you mind if I ask you some questions?”

The girl looked unimpressed. “They don’t pay me enough to answer questions.”

Michael set a red Gatorade and a bag of Hot Fries in front of her. “Aw, come on,” he said sweetly, flashing those killer dimples. “Just one or two questions?”

She started to ring it up. “Fine. But don’t take too long. I’m taking my break in five.”

Rylie rolled her eyes. Of course his charm worked even with sulky teenagers. “Do you work here every night?”

She nodded. “Unfortunately.”

Michael raised an eyebrow. “Young girl like you? Can that be safe?”

She handed him his change. “I have Spike to help me out.”

Rylie looked around. She hadn’t seen a dog when she walked in. If it was here, it was awfully well-behaved. “Spike?” Michael asked, taking the word out of her mouth.

“Yeah.” She reached behind the desk, pulled out an extra-large canister of Mace, and pointed it at him, finger on trigger.

The agents both stepped back. “Okay. Whoa,” Michael said to defuse the situation. “Easy with that.”

She put it back. “But yes, I’m here every night. It’s probably against child labor laws. But you’d have to take that up with my parents.”

“Ah,” Rylie said. “So your parents own the place?”

“Last I checked,” she said, staring at her black-painted fingernails. “If I’m not working here, I’m usually hanging around here. Nothing else to do in this godforsaken rathole of a town. Except drugs.” She winced. “Whoops. Probably shouldn’t have said that. Considering you’re feds and all. What do you want to know?”

Michael said, “It’s all right. We just wanted to see if you’d seen a couple of people that might’ve come in before.” He pulled out the file photograph of Gary Blake, a pale kid with a messy mop of reddish hair and freckles.

The second she saw it, she nodded. “Yep. I saw him. The police asked me about him. He bought a Mountain Dew here. Told me he needed to stay awake for what he had planned.”

“Did he tell you what he had planned?” Rylie asked.

She shook her head. “No, but he came off the highway on foot. I saw that. And then he stood outside for a while, trying to bum a ride off someone.”

Rylie jumped on that. “He did? Did you see who he left with?”

“He didn’t leave with anyone. Eventually, when I realized what he was up to, I ran out there and chased him off. My parents don’t like people doing that. They think it scares customers away.” She shrugged. “So he just headed east. I remember him walking out there, thumb up.”

Michael asked, “So the last you saw him, he was alone?”

“Yep. I’m probably the last one who saw him alive, huh? He was murdered, huh?” She grinned sadistically. “Wicked.”

Michael couldn’t disguise the disgust on his face at that. “Yeah,” he mumbled, pulling another photograph out of the file. “What about this one? This would’ve been a couple nights ago, maybe.”

This time, Rylie expected a blank look. Instead, the girl nodded. “Oh, yeah, I saw her, too.”

“You did?” Michael asked, echoing Rylie’s surprise. “She came in here?”

“Uh-huh.” She grabbed a giant soda cup from behind the counter and lifted the straw to her lips, but didn’t take a sip. “She’s dead too? Wild! Like a serial killing?”

“We’re just investigating, and at this point, we’re not sure of any connection,” Rylie said. “Can you tell me what you remember about her?”

“Not much,” she said with a shrug. “She came in here pretty late at night, and I think she bought a candy bar and didn’t really talk to me. But… oh, wait.” Her eyes lit up.

They both leaned forward. “And?” Michael prompted.

“She was just like the other guy. Except she was going west. She stood outside, looking for someone to drive her there. Thought she’d found someone, but for whatever reason, that person went off without her. I don’t know why. I think they had a fight because she was upset. I thought she might be crying.” The girl gnawed on her lip. “I was going to tell her to leave, but I felt bad for her. And then she just walked off on her own, heading west on the highway.”

“Your parents…who are they?” Rylie asked. “Where do they live?”

“Abe and Mabel Whitford?” she said, as if she wasn’t sure. “We live in the trailer park down the street. About a mile from here. If I need anything, I just call my dad, and he comes right out. Do you want me to call him?”

Rylie shook her head. "At this point, it's all right. Have you seen any strange characters hanging around the area lately?"

She shook her head. "Well, strange types always come in here to fill up."

"But anyone lingering? Maybe here more than once?"

"No. Nothing like that. Most of the people I see know better than to come back to this dump."

"You have any security tapes for this place?" Michael said, looking up at the corners of the small room for a video camera.

She nodded. "Police took the first one. I can give you the one with the girl. It was two days ago?"

"Two or three. Yeah."

She reached behind the counter and pulled out two videotapes. "Not exactly cutting edge, but here you go."

"Thanks," Michael said. "You've been a big help."

Rylie thanked the girl, too, and they went outside. Rylie looked up and down the paved area in front of the gas station, wishing for some clue. But she found nothing.

In the darkness, Rylie could just see the highway, empty except for the lights of an odd car here or there, cutting through the darkness. Sometimes that highway reminded her of a big snake lying in wait, seemingly harmless, but with the potential to be lethal. "Well, now we know they were both here. That's another thing they have in common."

"But what does that tell us?" Michael said, popping open his drink and taking a long swig. He stuffed the bottle under his arm, opened the Hot Fries, and held them out to her. "Fry?"

She shook her head, wrinkling her nose. Now her truck would probably smell like Hot Fries for the rest of the night. Great. She had no idea how he could stomach that junk. "It tells us… not that much. But maybe this is where the killer picks his victims from. Maybe he stays here, close by, but out of reach, and watches, looking for someone who is desperate."

"That cashier didn't see anyone."

She motioned to the videos, which she'd set on the center console. "Maybe we'll see otherwise on there. It's worth a shot."

He smirked. "Okay, so… we're going back to headquarters right now to check that out?"

"Don't you think we should? The killer could be out there right now, trying to find another victim."

He sighed. "Yeah. Let's go."

She knew he'd say that. As long a day as it had been, as much as she knew he wanted to go and hit the hay back at Hoskins's house, he also wanted to find this killer as much as she did. So she pointed her car in the direction of Missoula, heading west on I-86.

CHAPTER TEN

The man sat in his car, parked in a distant corner of the gas station, peeling peanuts, popping them in his mouth, and watching the scene ahead of him. This area of Montana never got much traffic, but when it did, people usually stopped at this place.

He knew he had to be careful. He'd already killed twice, which meant that the police were probably scratching their heads, wondering if the murders were connected. But so far, he hadn't seen much of an uptick in police presence around the places he frequented. It was likely that they were leaning toward the similarities in the murders being a coincidence.

If he dared to pick up another hitchhiker, that would definitely swing opinion the other way. Three similar murders in the area? That would certainly arouse suspicions.

He'd thought about moving out of the area. Going elsewhere. But he couldn't do that. This was where he had to stay.

This area held special significance. It was where she had died.

He'd also thought about stopping. But he couldn't do that either, any more than he could simply stop breathing. He hadn't expected to feel the way he had. The thrill of the first time? It was like nothing he'd ever experienced. It was as if she was holding his hand, guiding him, telling him this was right, something that needed to be done. The elation was something he didn't know possible. The second he came home and washed the blood from his hands, he only wanted more.

More revenge. For her.

So he'd taken his precautions. In this corner of the parking lot, cameras wouldn't catch him. He was out of sight of the cashier, too, so she probably wouldn't be able to notice him. Not that she'd remember him even if she did. He switched things up enough so he'd never get caught.

He took a swig of the giant coffee he'd brought from home. It was cold now. He'd been patrolling the interstate for the past few hours, waiting for his chance.

As he sat there, watching travelers fill up their cars, maybe stop inside for a coffee to keep them awake on their journeys, he noticed a figure walking along the overpass, on the shoulder of the road.

He shifted to get a better look, squinting through the darkness to see in the driver's side mirror.

It was a female, young, with long hair in two low pigtails that hung nearly to her waist. A bit of a hippie, she was wearing a floppy-rimmed hat, jeans, and a crochet top that bared her bellybutton. She had a bag slung over her shoulder and a placid smile on her face as she strode easily down the slope toward the gas station.

For a moment, he just sat there, agog. She looked almost exactly like *her*.

Luckily, he noticed her coming closer before she noticed him and powered up his window. Thank goodness for tinted windows. Standing right in front of his bumper, she didn't seem to notice him at all. She reached into her bag, grabbed a stack of dog-eared leaflets, and shoved one under his windshield wiper, not ever glancing his way, even though he was less than a foot away. Then she continued on toward the gas station.

A moment later, the man powered down his window and grabbed the leaflet. He stared at it:

BUT WHO DO YOU SAY I AM? The TRUTH about JESUS CHRIST—JESUS DIED FOR YOU, AND LIVES IN HEAVEN, WAITING FOR YOU!

He crumpled it in his fist as he watched the woman, practically skipping from car to car near the convenience store, leaving pamphlets on every car she came across. She went inside, and he watched her make a beeline to the cashier, handing her a brochure, as well. After that, she stepped outside and surveyed the area, likely wondering where else she could leave her gifts.

It was at that moment that a dark minivan pulled off the interstate and headed into the lot, parking at the gas pump nearest to the man. Weighed down by a hard, rooftop cargo box, toting along a rack full of bicycles of various sizes, wheels spinning, it slowed to a stop.

He watched as a middle-aged balding man in cargo shorts and a T-shirt hopped out. His wife, in the passenger seat, rolled down the window and they spoke. The man couldn't hear all of it, but he heard something about the bathroom and a hotel.

Probably that there wasn't another one for miles, and the hotel they'd planned to stay at was still pretty far down the road.

The wife, pretty, with red hair and pale skin, opened the door, then got out and slid back the side door for the back of the van. Three kids piled out, all with red hair and freckles like the mom. They marched into the convenience store, single file. When she saw the hippie, the woman stopped for a moment, shook her head, then ushered the kids inside.

Meanwhile, the father continued to fill up the car, watching the digital display as he cocked his hip, one hand on the nozzle. He didn't notice the blonde hippie approaching him until she was right across from him. When she spoke, he took a step back, surprised.

The man leaned forward, trying to glean something from their conversation. She pointed down the road. "… to Wyoming, at least. You think you can help me out?"

He shook his head and a bunch of excuses flooded out, but the only one the man could hear was "Car's too full with luggage as it is." The father patted the giant hard luggage rack attached to the top of the minivan. "Sorry."

"Are you sure? I don't take up much space," she said with a smile, just as the wife returned, a suspicious look on her face.

The wife motioned her off. "I'm sorry, but we really can't help you."

The girl looked up and down the road. "Oh, but I'm so tired. And it's getting so late. Don't you think you could—"

"I'm sorry," the man said, though not as firmly as he should have.

So of course, the girl continued to pester them, even as they loaded the children back in the car. The nerve of the woman. She kept on going with her pathetic sob story about why she needed to ride with them. The nice couple entertained her, apologizing up and down, but remaining firm.

No, the man decided. She was nothing like her.

His sister, Eloise, had been sweet and kind. She'd been gentle and friendly to everyone out there. But there were others out there, predators. And this girl was clearly one of those. She'd suck a person dry, take what she could get and leave them bleeding in the dust on the side of the road.

The man shook his head. The father probably didn't want to create a scene in front of the kids. But what he should've done was tell that bitch to take a hike.

He would have. He'd have grabbed her by the throat and made her scared. What right did she have to bother people like that? Did she think she owned the world?

Finally, the family finished piling into their car. As the father started the engine and it became clear the woman's coaxing wasn't working, her demeanor suddenly shifted.

"You're really going to freaking leave me here?" she shouted, shaking her fist at them. "Really? That's cruel. Jesus would help!"

They pulled off, stopping at the main road before continuing onto the highway. She gave them the middle-finger salute and shoved her brochures into her bag, mumbling under her breath. Then she reached down, adjusted her sandal, and headed in the direction of the highway on foot.

He smiled. Oh, yes, this was definitely shaping up to be his night.

He started his car and shifted into drive.

A little longer. He'd give her a bit of a head start, and then he'd follow.

CHAPTER ELEVEN

By the time Rylie pulled up at the precinct, it was almost ten in the evening. She'd been lagging, too, even with the coffee, so she rolled down the windows in the truck and let the cool air brace her.

They went inside to a skeleton crew of officers, all new faces from earlier that day. A guy Michael clearly didn't know was manning the front desk, because Michael pulled out his credentials and said, "We were here earlier. Do you have a VCR we can check out?"

The officer said, "What the hell is a VCR?"

Rylie looked at him. He was pretty young-looking, but after being called Mom by Brisbane, along with the fatigue, she felt like she was a thousand years old. She held up the tape. "For this?"

He squinted at it like he'd never seen it before.

"Can we take a look around in your back office?" she muttered.

He nodded and buzzed them through. As she walked down the hall, looking for a storage room, she said to Michael, "They've got to have one somewhere, if they checked out the other tape. Right?"

They pushed open a door to a storage closet, and among the old uniforms and other junk, found an old television set and VCR on a cart. "Aha," Michael said, helping her wheel it out.

Wheeling it back into the conference room, Michael set to getting it hooked up. When he finished, he slipped the tape in and scratched the side of his head. "I think I did that right."

Sure enough, the grainy image showed the front of the Gas Express in Clinton. The camera focused on the pumps in the lot, and the area right in front of the store. They watched for a little while, not speaking. "Fast forward," Rylie said.

Michael pressed the button and the images began to move in double time, cars zooming in, filling up, and leaving, people going in and out of the store. No one who fit the description of Candy Fronheiser.

But then a blonde girl appeared, walking toward the convenience store. "Stop!"

Michael did.

"Rewind."

He did so, and then started up again. Sure enough, the girl walked from the direction of the interstate, toward the convenience store. She hadn't arrived in a car. She spent a few minutes, out of the view of the camera. While she was in the store, another car pulled up, one of those old-model, seventies jobbies that was half car, half-pickup.

Michael stared at it as an obese man with a balding head and a mop of curls around his ears pulled his body out from the steering wheel. "Sweet ride."

"Are you kidding me? I always thought cars like that were so ugly."

"Blasphemy. That's a Chevy El Camino. They don't make cars like that anymore," he said, whistling.

"Thank God," she murmured, as they watched the large man insert the pump into his car, then stand there, leaning against his car as the tank filled.

As Candy left the convenience store, another car pulled up, and a young man got out. Candy spoke to him, but he shook his head and went inside.

"Look at that. Did you see that?" Rylie said, rewinding and playing it again. The man filling his tank had his eyes on her, following her the whole time. Even as she left, walking back toward the interstate, he craned his neck to watch her.

Michael crossed his arms and nodded. "The man might have a sweet ride, but he's definitely a creeper."

"You're telling me."

Shortly after, the creeper got into his car and drove off, putting on his blinker to head for the interstate. As his car came close to the camera, Rylie paused it. "There. His license plate."

"Can't read it."

They rewound, but it was too fuzzy to see it fully. "That's a definite bucking bronco in the center there, I think."

"And I think the last part is an I or a one." She found a couple of scattered napkins on the table and scribbled it down.

Michael took it from her. "Okay, dark blue Chevy El Camino with Wyoming license plates. Shouldn't be too much trouble. I'll see if Beaker can run this for us."

He rushed out, lifting his phone to his ear. Beaker was their IT genius, and though he was currently still in Rapid City, the man never slept. He'd be eager to help out on this, and would probably return the information they were looking for in record time.

Rylie leaned against the table, rewinding and starting the video again and again, trying to glean more information about this suspect. Maybe the other video, from Gary's appearance, had more, something the police might have missed. Maybe the cashier hadn't noticed it, but it was possible this man had been there then, too. Either way, he was the best shot they had.

A moment later, Michael came back, holding the same slip of paper in one hand, the phone in the other. "Got it. A guy named Ryan Hennessey. And get this. He might have a Wyoming license plate, but for the last six months, he's been living in a trailer park just south of Missoula."

That was promising. She jumped up. "Okay, I'm ready. Let's do this."

They rushed out to the car and Michael plugged the address into her GPS. She pulled out of the department lot, and moments later, she knew exactly where they were. They were cruising down Missoula's main drag, heading straight for I-86.

It turned out Ryan Hennessey's trailer complex was a mere stone's throw from the interstate. The park was vast, but save for the lights on in some individual mobile homes, there was only one light on at the entrance, illuminating a sign that said *Tuckahoe Estates.* Most of the homes hulked in complete darkness. Even the office looked deserted.

Rylie squinted. "How are we supposed to find his?"

He checked the paper. "Number 128." Grabbing the flashlight on his phone, he shined the light on one of the mobile homes, with black-and-white awnings and potted plants everywhere. The number was 34.

She drove on, but the next one was 43. "They're not in any great order. Maybe we should've stopped in at the office and asked."

"It didn't look like anyone was there," Michael said, motioning to the nearest one that was lit up. An old lady in a housecoat was sitting in a lounge chair outside, smoking a cigarette. He powered down the window. "Hi, ma'am."

She just stared straight ahead, and not directly at him.

"Excuse me, ma'am?" he tried again.

It didn't help. She didn't move a muscle. Michael groaned. Rylie chuckled. *Looks like he finally found a woman who's immune to his charm.*

The next time he spoke, it was a yell, so loud that dogs nearby began to bark. "Hello! Excuse me!"

She blinked. "I hear you. I'm not deaf. What do you want?" she muttered.

"Could've fooled me," he muttered under his breath, before calling, "Can you direct us to Ryan Hennessey's place?"

"Who?"

He glanced down at the paper. "Number 128."

She motioned him off with a flick of her hand. "The one hundreds are in the back. Near the highway."

Rylie took off before he could even thank her. This was sounding more promising than ever. Ryan's home backed up to the highway. He probably saw hitchhikers walking the road all the time. Maybe they'd annoyed him, trespassing on his land, and he'd snapped. Or maybe he'd just taken advantage of the opportunity—people, all alone and desperate for the kindness of strangers. Whatever it was, his home was ideally situated to give him access to these travelers.

She was so busy thinking up wild theories as to why Ryan had killed that she didn't realize she was going fast until she hit a bump so hard it made her teeth rattle.

"Whoa, slow down. Speed limit's five in here," Michael warned.

"We're almost there," she said, lowering her speed to twenty. "Look."

They reached a T intersection with a chain-link fence in front of them. It was all that separated them from the interstate. At the T, she turned right, and Michael shined the flashlight on the trailers. "One-twenty-four. One-twenty-seven. That one. The last one in the aisle."

He pointed at a trailer in the very corner of the property, pushed up against a hill. A bare, unadorned rectangle with no homey touches, unless you counted the beer bottles in a garbage can out front, it screamed "single male." It was definitely one of the more secluded of the homesites, set away from the others, and yet it still had a good view of the highway.

But all the windows were dark. As Michael arced the flashlight over it, he shook his head. "Looks like he's not here. His car isn't here, that's for sure."

Rylie pulled up in front and unsnapped her seatbelt anyway. They were here. They might as well check.

She climbed out of the car and went to the small side door, banging on it, then on the window. There was no answer. "Mr. Hennessey?" she called. "It's the FBI. Just want to ask you some questions."

No one answered. She stood on her toes and peered in the windows, hoping for some clues. Moonlight revealed that every surface in the small kitchenette was cluttered with food items—peanut butter jars, boxes of crackers, soda and beer cans. He was definitely a slob, but that didn't make him a criminal.

When she turned back, she saw Michael picking through the garbage can. "Anything?"

He shook his head. "Not that I can tell."

She sighed and looked around. "Damn."

At that moment, fatigue overcame her. She yawned.

"I guess we should call it a night, huh? Let's call in one of the cops on duty and ask them to keep an eye on the place."

He gave a double thumbs-up. "We'll come back here tomorrow morning. Maybe he'll be back."

Or maybe he's out right now, killing his next victim. She couldn't shake the thought from her head. As she got into the car, she said, "Can you call your buddies and tell them to keep an eye out for his car and to call us if they have a sighting?"

"Yep." He pulled his phone out. "Will do."

She slowly found her way out of the maze of paths that made up the RV park, and got on the main road leading to the interstate.

As they passed the gas station on the way to the ramp, Rylie eyed the place, hoping everyone there would be safe. As Michael chatted on with a Missoula officer, she stared at the many travelers under the lights of the station, hoping they all had gotten the warning from the police about hitchhiking. Not that it would help. Hitchhiking had always been prohibited, and yet people still did it. Desperate people with no other way to get where they wanted to be.

So that meant there was still danger out there. Danger that would persist until they caught the guy.

She was just about to turn her attention toward the ramp when she saw it. Lifting her foot off the gas, she said, "Michael?"

"Huh?" he said, pulling the phone down from his ear. "They're going to put an APB out on that—"

"Michael." She pointed across the street toward the gas station. "Is that what I think it is?"

He leaned forward and squinted. "Yeah. That's the El Camino we're looking for."

She slammed on the brakes and swerved into the left lane. *Ryan Hennessey, here we come.*

CHAPTER TWELVE

Rylie cut across the opposing traffic lane and pulled her pickup truck into the gas station's parking lot in a hurry. The closer they got, the better this looked. The car was parked at a pump, but the driver was nowhere in sight.

As they pulled up behind it, they saw Ryan Hennessey appearing from the convenience store. He was wearing a too-tight T-shirt that didn't quite cover his massive belly, and his jeans were hung so low that they dragged on the ground over his Birks. His bald spot was covered by a Colorado Rockies cap, and a mop of curls hung in his eyes. Oblivious to them, he sauntered toward his car, keys in hand, sipping from an extra-huge drink cup.

They got out and approached him, one on each side of his car.

As they neared his back bumper, Michael shouted, "Hennessey! FBI!"

Quicker than either of them had expected, he dropped his drink and jumped into his car, starting the engine and peeling off. Rylie drew her gun too late. There were people in the way, and she wouldn't get in a clean shot.

She rushed to the truck. "Bris! Come on!" she shouted, throwing herself in, plunging the key into the ignition, and starting the engine in one swift movement.

Hennessey swerved onto the street and went under the underpass for the interstate. Rylie peeled out onto the street, following close behind. The road was empty, like so many in this area, nothing but hilly plains stretching out into the darkness. Dust clouded up around her and insects pinged the windshield as she floored the gas, right on the guy's tail.

"You're gonna do something crazy, aren't you?" Michael said, holding on to the strap over the passenger-side door.

"I need to stop him," she said in a low, calm voice, tightening her fingers on the steering wheel. She wasn't sure what she'd do, but she knew one thing—it would be whatever she needed to do in order to stop him.

"Yeah… but don't get us killed—" Hennessey suddenly banked left, so she swerved and did the same, making Michael put his foot up on the dashboard. "Look out!"

She corrected just in time to avoid plunging off the road into a ravine. The truck fishtailing, she found her place on the road and surged ahead. Michael was a sissy when it came to driving. She knew that already. If this had been his truck, they would've likely lost Hennessey already.

But Rylie didn't care. She would catch up with this guy. Or else.

He hung another left onto a dirt road, and she followed. She floored the gas pedal again, clinging tight to his back bumper.

"You're going to do it, aren't you?" Michael groaned through gritted teeth.

"Do what?"

"The pit maneuver."

She tried it before, with a semi. That hadn't worked out so well. But this was a no-brainer. Hennessey was driving a pathetic little half-truck. It'd work great, if she could just get close enough to—

"But it's a sweet ride!" Michael shouted as she brought her front bumper just close enough to the El Camino and did a quick turn of the steering wheel. Bracing herself, she corrected easily, while the car in front of her spun out, consumed in a cloud of dust.

She slammed on the brakes and searched through the haze. "Did it w—" She stopped when she heard tires squealing and the definite, sickening crunch of a car crashing not too far away. When she jumped out of the truck, the dust was already settling, and the "sweet ride" was lying in a ditch, its front end smashed in.

As they jogged up to meet it, the front door opened. The first thing Rylie heard was the sound of heavy breathing.

Ryan Hennessey was hyperventilating.

She stood on the mound as he pulled himself out and slunk to the ground, breathing hard.

"Hey, man," Michael said, watching him. "You okay?"

He grasped at his heart. "I can't breathe. I can't—"

Rylie rolled her eyes, but Michael, as usual, was more compassionate, pulling his phone from his pocket. "Stay right there. I'm calling an ambulance."

Rylie leaned over the man, who already seemed better, as he slumped there, his breathing returning to normal. "Why the hell did you run away?"

"I—I don't know," he said between gasps. "You just called my name. All I saw were two people running for me. Thought I was in trouble. That's it."

"You're in trouble," she said. "Now. Before, we just wanted to talk to you. When someone identifies themselves as the FBI, you don't run."

He nodded sullenly. "All right. All right. What's this about? I didn't do nothing wrong."

"We want to talk to you in connection with the disappearance of a girl who was last seen at the Clinton Gas Express a couple days ago. Her name was Candy Fronheiser," she said. "You pick up any hitchhikers recently?"

His eyes went wide. He slumped over. "I can't—I can't breathe—"

Michael ended the call and said, "Ambulance is on the way. Looks like that sweet ride is in pretty bad shape."

He went around the front to take a look at it, and Rylie moved forward, ready to cuff their suspect. As she stood there, feeling in the pocket of her jacket, she realized she didn't have a pair of cuffs. "Hey, Bris, do you have—"

Before she could say more, a fist hit her square in the jaw, sending her stumbling back, vision swimming. By the time her backside hit the ground, she'd already realized her mistake. She'd been suckered by that jerk, and now he was lumbering across the grassy plain, trying to get away from them.

Tasting blood, she wiped at the side of her mouth and found it dripping from her lips as she called, "Bris!"

She scrambled to her feet, her focus off, making her see double of everything, and ran after him. But her partner caught sight of him and took after him. Hennessey might have been faking the heart attack, but he wasn't in good shape. He didn't make it far before Michael caught up with him, yanking him by the back of his T-shirt and pulling him back like a yo-yo on a string. When Hennessey reeled back, Michael leveled him with a single punch to the face. He fell down flat, out cold.

Rylie's vision returned as she rushed up to meet him. Standing over the man's motionless body, he looked over at her. "You okay, Wolf?"

"Fine." She licked the blood from her lips as the sound of the sirens wailed in the distance. As glad as she was that Hennessey had been disarmed, she wished she'd been the one to do it. "He's our guy. I know it. I guess we'll have to interview him in the hospital."

“Guess so,” Michael muttered, yawning as he snapped a pair of handcuffs on their suspect. The ambulance drew near, and she waved it down.

She knew he must’ve been exhausted, as much as he wasn’t saying so. She was, too. They’d been chugging coffee, but all that driving and running back and forth had taken its toll. It was now after eleven, and Hoskins was probably wondering where they hell they’d gone off to.

But if they could put this case to bed tonight and sleep soundly, it would be worth it. She told herself that and forced her eyes open as she greeted the EMTs.

CHAPTER THIRTEEN

Rylie sipped cold coffee as she waited in the hallway of the Western Montana Medical Center for the doctors to finish with their latest suspect. As she did, she tapped her foot impatiently on the ground and kept checking the time. Now it was after midnight.

Michael came down the hall with two fresh cups of coffee, handing her one and taking the cold one away. "Don't worry, killer. You'll get your chance with him soon."

She sighed. "I wonder if he's pulling the heart-attack ruse with them, too. He's totally shifty. Definitely has something to hide."

He nodded. "Yeah. But…"

Rylie didn't like that. He sounded almost doubtful. Where did that come from? After what he'd done? "But what? You saw what he did."

"Yeah. I know. But I called the precinct and asked them to queue up the surveillance video from when Gary Blake disappeared. They did…"

Her eyes shot to meet his. He was hesitating. That wasn't good. "And?"

"And they didn't see an El Camino. At all, that night. At least, it wasn't on the video."

She shrugged. "Well, that doesn't mean anything. He might have picked him up somewhere else."

He nodded. "Yeah, yeah. Right. Just wanted you to be aware."

She sipped the new coffee, forgetting how hot it was, and scalded her tongue. If this guy wasn't the killer, all it meant was they were back at square one. No leads. And no going back east…

"How's your mouth?" he said, pointing to her jaw.

"It's fine. It's nothing," she said, waving him away. "Stop obsessing."

He shrugged and mumbled, "Doesn't look like nothing."

What was that supposed to mean? She stalked down the hall, and lacking a mirror, peered in the shiny metal side of a utility cart. Her jaw was starting to swell *bad*. It was turning colors not seen in nature, a gray-purple. She opened her mouth wider and felt it. Okay, so it wasn't the greatest.

"Here," Michael said. When she turned, he had an icepack, which he gently lifted up to her jaw. She put her hand on it, taking it from him, but still he stayed there for what seemed like a beat too long, staring down at her. Her face started to heat. "You'll be back to normal in no time."

"Thanks," she mumbled, breaking eye contact and practically yanking herself away. If she was blushing, she didn't want him to see.

Luckily, a male doctor stepped into the hallway, dispelling the awkwardness of the moment. He looked over at her from the rims of his bifocals. "Agent? You can go in and speak with him."

"Is he all right?" Michael asked.

"It seems so. Just a mild concussion. He's awake now, just a little woozy. What he needs is rest."

"No heart defects?" Rylie asked, unable to hide her sarcasm as she headed for the door to his room. "What a surprise."

Michael elbowed her. "You're brutal."

She pointed to her bulging jaw. "*I'm* brutal?"

"Yeah. Guess you have a point."

They went inside to find the man sitting up in bed, eyes bleary. He had a bruise on his cheek that rivaled Rylie's. His head lolled as he watched them come in, and he shook his head. "I don't wanna talk. I don't want to—"

"You have to," she said, crossing her arms. "We're done playing nice with you, Hennessey. You need to answer for where you were two nights ago. Did you pick up a hitchhiker?"

He stared. "Uh… I don't remember," he finally said, sheepish.

"Bullshit," Rylie said. "We have you on tape at the same time as Candy Fronheiser, who was found murdered. That was the last place she was seen alive. So we need to know what you know."

He blinked. "I swear. I didn't do it."

Michael grabbed a chair and dragged it over to the bedside. "All right. But you were there." He motioned to Rylie, who produced the photograph of Candy from the file. Michael held it in front of Ryan. "Do you remember her?"

His Adam's apple bobbed as he swallowed. "She's dead?"

"Yeah. So what can you tell me?"

He sighed. "I talked to her. At the gas station, yeah. And I told her that I'd give her a ride if she wanted one. She told me to buzz off."

"And that was it?"

He stared down at his hands, crossed over his protruding belly. "Maybe not. I followed her. I got back on the road and saw her walking. I thought that maybe, since she didn't get a better offer, she'd reconsider. So I followed her along the road a little bit, trying to convince her. She kept saying no. And so then I rode off. I swear. That was the last time I saw her, in my rearview mirror."

Rylie frowned. "You do that a lot, do you? Try to pick up hitchhiking women?"

He shrugged. "I try to be helpful."

Right. He tries to get himself some play the only way he knows how, she thought. She couldn't imagine a guy like him had girls beating down his door. Maybe he had to fight with them. And maybe he took it too far—

"What about last week. Say, mid-week? Can you account for your movements then?" Michael asked.

He nodded. "I was with my brother in Cheyenne all last week. Helping him prepare for the rodeo."

"You were?" He glanced at Rylie, who frowned. "And he'll back up your story? Anyone else?"

"*Everyone* else." He reached for his phone on the table and opened it up, then showed them a photograph of a him and a couple of cowboys in front of the famous Cheyenne Frontier Days sign. Rylie scrolled through. The time stamps went all week.

She gnawed on her lip. If Ryan Hennessey was there in Wyoming, then he couldn't have killed Gary Blake. Which meant… what did she have? Just a description of a guy in a sportscar who'd harassed Lottie on I-86…

But just then, Lottie's words came to her. *I couldn't see him very well. He just had thick hands. A deep voice. And I think, from his shadow, thick curly hair. But that's all I know.*

Rylie scrutinized the man in front of her, a sinking feeling growing in her stomach.

Thick hands. Check.

Deep voice. Check.

Thick, curly hair. Check.

She rolled her eyes to the ceiling. So even the description she had of the killer was probably wrong. Lottie's guy wasn't the killer. He was just some perv out for a good time. "Were you out last night, trying to pick up girls, too?"

He gave her a look so innocent, it was practically dripping with guilt.

She let out a growl and stalked out of the room.

Michael followed, soon after. "Hey. What's up?"

"That's not our guy. He's just some perv who likes picking up girls. He's the guy who tried to pick up Lottie, obviously."

The thought clearly hadn't occurred to Michael, because he muttered a curse under his breath. "That's right. All right, well. Tomorrow is a new day."

"And we have absolutely nothing to go on," she said through gritted teeth.

"We'll get something."

She hoped he was right. Her jaw was starting to ache, she was exhausted, and she felt like she'd just wasted an entire day of precious time. But it was time to stick a fork in this day and try to regroup for tomorrow. "Let's go get some rest."

*

Unfortunately, Hoskins's home wasn't quite as big and luxurious as Michael had made it seem.

In fact, it was only slightly larger than her one-bedroom apartment in Rapid City, and she'd thought that was pretty cramped and spartan. Hoskins's condo was a two-story building with two bedrooms, one bath. When they lugged their bags inside the darkened home and confirmed that fact, Brisbane rubbed the back of his neck, embarrassed.

"My bad. I should've known," he whispered, as Hoskins's snores emanated from the bedroom at the end of the hall. "Hoskins grew up with twelve brothers and sisters. So I guess this is like a giant palace to him."

"Hmm," she said, too tired to complain.

He pushed open the door for the guest bedroom and turned on the light. There was a nice queen bed there. The moment she laid eyes on it, she longed to sink into it and close her eyes.

The usual Brisbane would've made some flirty joke about sharing. But he must've been really tired, because he simply said, "You take this."

She gave him a look like, *Obviously.* But then she felt bad. "What about you?"

"That sofa out in the living room is calling my name."

"All right." She stepped inside and started to close the door. "Good night, Bris."

"Night," he said, from somewhere in the darkness down the hall.

She closed the door, sat down on the edge of the bed, and sighed. So much had happened in only twenty-four hours. She'd found a clue that had opened a door to her sister's disappearance she'd thought had been closed for good. She'd learned that her old boss was just waiting for her to fail, from half a country away. And she'd also found out that Michael Brisbane, who sometimes made her heart flutter in ways it definitely shouldn't, thought of her as a motherly figure.

But one thing that hadn't happened? They hadn't gotten any closer to finding out who had murdered those two hitchhikers.

Like Michael said, tomorrow was another day. Tomorrow, she'd make progress and get closer to finding the answers so she could go back east, to Elephant Hole, and possibly answer that burning question: What had happened to Maren Wolf?

The thought made her stomach churn with excitement and anxiety. What if, when she got there, she found nothing?

Or even more frightening… what if she found the answers she'd been waiting for, and they confirmed her worst fears?

CHAPTER FOURTEEN

The man smiled as he headed down I-86 toward Bearmouth. Every so often, he peered into the back seat at the girl trembling there, and his smile widened.

Her name was Eileen Devers. Only nineteen. She was from Colorado Springs. She'd been all over, supposedly, on a grand hitchhiking trip, first east, and now heading west. The things he had gleaned from her during the last half hour had been interesting indeed. She was someone who believed in light overpowering darkness.

As he tapped his fingers on the door, he wondered if tonight would change her mind.

But she was a predator, all the same. Oh, maybe she didn't act it yet, but one day, she would. She'd destroy. They all destroyed.

"It's for your own good, Eileen," he said to her, breaking the silence. "It can be dangerous out there. Especially a young girl like you, hitchhiking. Didn't your parents ever tell you that?"

The girl shrugged defiantly as she looked out the window, just as Eloise had when their parents had said hitchhiking was dangerous. She'd raised her hands and was now nervously braiding one of her long pigtails. "I don't care. I'm spreading the word of Jesus. Many have suffered to do so. The laws of his kingdom supersede the laws here on earth."

His top lip lifted into a snarl. She thought she could use that religious bullshit to justify her actions. He wasn't buying it. "Is that what you think?"

"It's what I know," she said, jutting her chin into the air.

"Interesting," he said, stroking his chin thoughtfully. "And where were you headed?"

"California. And beyond. I'm spreading the good word as far as I can. And someone like you is not going to stop me. Believe me. I'll keep going."

He chuckled to himself. "Is that so?"

"Definitely. His word will not be silenced."

He watched her in the back seat, staring out the window, undaunted. Sure, she'd spread the word of Jesus. And if someone didn't listen, she'd beat it into them. That's the way these people were. She needed to be pulled down a peg. And he knew just how to do it.

It was after midnight now, and the road stretched on before him. Despite this being the busiest road in southwestern Montana, he hadn't passed another car in at least five minutes. There was no one around, and so he decided the time had come.

He pulled to the side of the road, by a wooden railing over a small ravine. As the gravel pinged against the underside of his car, he heard the springs in the back seat shift, and felt Eileen tensing behind him. When the brakes squealed and he slowed to a stop she sat upright. "What are we doing here?"

He chuckled. "What can I say? Maybe I've had a change of heart."

Her eyes were full of doubt. "You have?"

He turned to find young Eileen eyeing him doubtfully. "Sure. I mean, your spirit has really shone through. We can't be right all the time. And maybe your light is needed elsewhere."

"Really?" She looked down at her bound hands. "So..."

"One moment." He slipped out of the car and went around the back of it, checking furtively to make sure his weapon was still at his hip. It was. He opened the back door and stooped to smile at her, then loosened the restraints.

She rubbed her wrists and said, "Thank you. I don't know how to—
"

"Not at all."

She slipped out of the car, straightened, and looked up and down the highway. When she turned to grab her bag, he took hold of his bully stick, hefting it in front of him.

When she whirled, he cracked her on the side of the skull. Easy, quick. Barely a flick of the wrist.

The result wasn't instant. Her face was completely blank for a moment, even as the blood started to trickle down her temple, coursing over her cheek and dripping from the edge of her chin.

"What..." she said dumbly, her eyes fastening on the weapon in his fist. "Why did you..."

The danger seemed to occur to her in a rush, and without another second's hesitation, she turned away from him, to run. But the open door of the car was in her way. She ran straight into it, letting out a muffled cry.

As she gripped the door frame, struggling to pull her body around it, he moved forward at a leisurely pace. He struck again, this time at the very crown of her head. She'd just gotten free of the door, but she managed only one step before stumbling to her knees on the gravel. She fell forward on her hands, then collapsed fully to the ground.

The man reached into his pocket and pulled out the rope. He looked up and down the road. No one. Perfect.

Strolling forward, he stood beside the body and crouched down. Despite her bloodied face, her still position, her eyelids were working to stay open. Her mouth opened, and out spilled one word, in only a breath. "Please…"

Poor Eileen Devers. Brought up to believe that where there was light, there could not be darkness. Wasn't that what the church said? But no one had told her that that wasn't always true. Sometimes, the blackest parts of the human soul were enough to extinguish even the hottest flame.

Sometimes, no matter what a person did, the darkness won.

CHAPTER FIFTEEN

"Hey," a voice said, stirring Rylie from a deep sleep.

She cracked an eyelid to find she was sitting in the top bunk bed in the RV, the flowered sheet piled up around her face. Beyond that, a girl with messy dark hair stood in front of the kitchenette, flour in her hair and a mischievous smile on her face.

Maren. Rylie's heart twisted at the sight of her big sister standing there, in bike shorts and a tank top that bared her flat stomach. Maren scratched her shin with the toes of her other foot and held up a spoon. "Are you going to help me or not? Or are you just going to sleep there all summer?"

Rylie sat up at once. Maren was a little annoyed with her, but she didn't care. She wanted to throw herself in her big sister's arms. But when she threw her feet over the side of the bed and jumped down, Maren stepped away.

She held out a bowl to her, full of flour. "Come on. Put the water in. Not too much."

"What are we making?" Rylie said, still dazed.

"A giant pancake. I want to make a huge one that takes up the whole griddle. We can share," she said with a sly grin. "But hurry. The others only went to the store. They'll be back any minute."

"Oh, okay," Rylie said, jumping into action. She poured the water, then stirred it up while Maren adjusted the temperature on the electric griddle. Rylie smiled. Her big sister was always doing things like this, coming up with crazy ideas she wanted to put in motion. And though there were three years separating them, it didn't matter to Maren. Rylie was her equal, her partner in crime.

Though the bowl was heavy with batter, together they poured it out so that it spread to cover the entire pan. "This is going to be epic!" Maren announced.

Rylie nodded, excited. She could almost taste it, the thick cake, the maple syrup, the butter…

"I've got to go," Maren said suddenly, heading for the door. "Keeping checking on it, okay? Don't let it burn."

Rylie's heart jumped into her throat. "Wait! Where are you—"

She reached for Maren's hand, but her sister pulled it free. "It's okay. I won't be gone long," she said, smiling. "And if I am, you can find me. You'll know where to look…"

The smell of something burning hit her nostrils, just as thick, gray smoke invaded. It accompanied the sound of the RV's front door slamming, so loud that it sounded like thunder—"

Rylie sat straight up in bed and realized someone was sitting next to her. Heart pounding, she searched the darkness to find Michael there, wearing nothing but loose gym shorts, his dark hair wayward on his head.

All at once, these many things that did not compute assaulted her. Where was Maren? What happened to the RV? Why was her partner sitting here on the edge of her bed?

"What—what are you doing here?" she whispered, pulling her sheets up to her chest, as if that would keep her modest. Not that it mattered, she was wearing an old FBI T-shirt and was perfectly decent.

"Sorry. I knocked. You didn't answer. You must've been out."

After the night before, did he blame her? "What's going on? What time is it?"

"It's a little after four. We just got a call from the precinct."

We? She blinked in the darkness, her eyes slowly adjusting to the pre-dawn purple haze filtering in from the blinds, and saw Hoskins standing in the doorway, dressed in a jacket and slacks. It instantly put her on high alert. "What is it?"

"They found another body. Near Bearmouth again."

Oh no. Her heart rate, which had been slowing, jumped again. She scrubbed her hands down her face, trying to get her eyes to cooperate with the rest of her body. "Another hitchhiker?"

"It appears so. Female. She was just left on the side of the road. No attempt made to hide her this time. That's all I know," Hoskins said. "I'm headed there now."

Michael nodded at him. "We'll be right with you."

Hoskins left, and Rylie jumped out of bed, diving for her duffel bag so she could grab some clean clothes. "Dammit. I knew we should've—"

"Read his mind?" Michael asked, standing up. "We were up most of the night, trying to figure things out. We did everything we could, Wolf. But we can't anticipate—"

"We should've done more," she said quietly, gathering up a pair of slacks and a plain white T-shirt to wear underneath her jacket. "Because we didn't do enough. Excuse me, I've got to get changed—"

He stopped her by laying a hand on her arm. When she looked down at it, he didn't let go. In fact, his grip seemed to tighten. He was so close that everywhere she looked, his bare chest was *right there*. The safest place to look, strangely enough, was right into his eyes.

Their gazes met and locked, but he didn't say anything for a beat.

"What?" she asked.

"You'll drive yourself crazy, Wolf, if you think you're supposed to be some kind of superhuman force that can anticipate these people's every move," he finally said. "One thing you should know from your training is that while we can analyze behavior to a point, you can't predict everything. If we did know everything about what made these people tick, we'd probably be out of a job by now."

She nodded. Yes, as usual, he had a point. It was something she told herself almost every day. But at times like this, when they'd been so close, only to let a killer slip through their fingers, she couldn't help feeling responsible. "All right. Let me get ready."

She went out into the bathroom across the hall, shivering a little as she turned on the light and recalled the dream. Maren. She'd felt so real. Funny, it'd been twenty years since they'd hung out like sisters together, and in the dream, it had felt so right. So natural. What would her life have been like if she'd grown up with Maren?

It was silly to think about. That day at Story Creek happened, and nothing she did could make it unhappen.

But she could find answers.

First things first, though. She had to concentrate on this case. Maren's case was cold. This one needed her most. And this time, the body was practically still warm. If they hurried, they'd be able to get to the crime scene and investigate from the very beginning.

She changed into her clothes in record time, splashed water on her face, brushed her teeth, finger combed her hair, and she was ready.

*

It wasn't hard to find the scene of the crime. It was barely dawn, and the lights of two police cars and an ambulance blazed through the darkness on the side of I-86. A massive semi from one of the big national trucking companies was also parked on the side of the road, farther up on the shoulder. Several people were standing on the edge of the road. Rylie recognized some of the officers as Brisbane's friends whom she'd met the day before. Hoskins was also there, talking to a man in a trucker cap, probably the witness.

Bile rose in Rylie's throat as she took in the scene. They'd been right here yesterday. They'd passed this place several times. And yet—

She stopped herself. *Michael's right. You can't anticipate. There was nothing you could have done.*

Michael squinted through the windshield. He looked half-asleep, too. They probably should've stopped for coffee, like he'd wanted to, but she hadn't wanted to waste the time. "Was I dreaming it, or did Hoskins say the murderer killed her right here on the side of the road?" he asked.

She pulled off her seatbelt as she studied the scene in the growing light of dawn, spreading itself over the barren landscape, painting it a warm, burnt sienna. "I think so."

"Got to have some balls to pull that out in the open, don't you think?"

She didn't answer. She was already stepping out to join the others and find out more. What had they missed? Where had this girl come from? Did he leave behind any clues this time? The questions beat at her brain, making her hands shake as she stepped into the circle that had gathered around the body. "What do we have here?"

They all turned to look at her. She glared. Had they forgotten who she was already?

Michael joined the group, shaking hands all around, a reminder that she'd forgotten to ease her way into the situation. Oh, that was it. But she couldn't help it. She was going on too little sleep, and was too antsy, to make small talk.

There was a dead body there, lying face down, her long, russet-colored hair half-braided. Her bare arms were spread out at her sides. She was wearing jeans and sandals, and scattered around her were a number of pamphlets.

Hoskins said, "Her name is Eileen Devers. Again, she wasn't robbed. All of her things were found right with her. She was hit over the head with some kind of blunt instrument, then strangled and left here. From what we can tell, it all happened right here. We've got tire tracks and footprints. The ones that don't belong to her are a typical men's size ten. That doesn't narrow things down a whole lot."

Rylie stooped to pick up one of the brochures. On the front was a crudely drawn picture of Jesus on the cross.

"Looks like she was probably hiking from place to place, evangelizing. And once again, probably picked the wrong person to hitch a ride with," Hoskins said.

"Any other evidence left behind?" Michael said, crouching in the road and checking it out.

Hoskins shook his head.

Rylie crouched over the girl again as the photographer snapped pictures. She noticed something on the girl's wrist that looked like a small bruise. "Take a photo of that, please," she instructed photographer.

"What is it?" Hoskins said.

"Bruising. Looks like she might've been restrained before she was killed."

Michael looked around. "If that's the case, where are the restraints?"

Rylie followed her partner and scanned the scene herself, using a flashlight. "Who found the body?"

The detective motioned to a rail-thin, older man in a trucker's cap who was leaning against the wooden railing, smoking a cigarette. He looked a bit stunned.

She went over to him. "Hi, I'm Rylie Wolf from the FBI. You found the body?"

"Yeah." He reached out a hand to shake hers. "I'm up and down this road at least three times a week on the way to Boise. I know it like the back of my hand. So when I see something wrong, I notice it."

"What did you see?"

Michael joined her just as the man, shuddering, said, "I saw a lump on the side of the road. My headlights lit it up, and at first I thought it was nothing but a pile of trash someone had left behind. But then I saw the blood. The skin. I pulled over and went to see if she was okay. She wasn't breathing, but she was warm. Like it just happened."

Like it just happened. Once again, Rylie found herself wishing she hadn't given in and decided to call it a day. If they'd stayed out on the beat, maybe…

She forced those thoughts away as Michael said, "What time was this, you said?"

"Just about an hour ago. Three-thirty? I work overnights, when it's less crowded, and sleep in the day. I live in Boise."

Michael nodded. "Did you see anyone else on the road tonight while you were driving? Maybe someone behaving strangely?"

The trucker shook his head. "Just the same old people. Some people just leisurely driving. Others too in a rush to get where they're going. No one who really stands out."

Rylie let out a sigh and returned to the body as it was loaded up onto the stretcher to be taken away. She'd hoped that with a body there, she'd have more to go on, a better clue as to who could've done this. But as she scanned the faces of the other officers in the area, only one thing seemed clear—they were still in the dark.

No. There had to be something. She just needed to think about this.

She stared at the tire tracks. Hoskins and the other officers were in a circle, talking. One of them laughed, which annoyed her. How could they be sitting around, gossiping like co-workers around the water cooler, when someone had died?

"Hey, Hoskins," she shouted.

He turned and looked at her, confusion on his face. "Huh?"

"Are these tire tracks being analyzed?"

"Yeah, we've taken photographs. But from what we can tell, looks like a pretty popular model. And it doesn't match any of the tracks near any of the other murders."

She raised an eyebrow. Odd that he knew that, considering the murder just happened. "How do you know that?"

He rolled his eyes. "Because there were no tire tracks at Gary Blake's murder. And the ones at Candy Fronheiser's were thick. Like truck tires. Those are car tires."

That was interesting. There was a possibility the tire tracks were from some random car that had parked in the area of Candy's dumping, and not from the car of the murderer. But if they'd both belonged to the murderer, that meant he'd dumped his car, too, before going off on the hunt again. It meant he was really trying to cover his tracks.

Still crouching, she frog-walked along the shoulder, studying the footprints belonging to the girl, Eileen. They seemed to disappear right where the car's tires were. She scanned farther back on the road, shining her flashlight along the shoulder, trying to find more prints belonging to the victim. But there were none.

Michael was talking with his buddies, but when Rylie snapped her fingers, he jogged over. "What's up? You find something?"

“Yeah. Well, I don’t know,” she said, pointing to the girl’s footprints. “Look at the way they’re facing here. Away from the road. Beside the tire tracks. And then here.”

He fisted his hands on his hips. “Yeah. So?”

“But they’re not over here…” She pointed down the road. “Anywhere down there. Do you see them?”

He blinked. “Wait, so…”

“She was attacked. Right here by the car. But she wasn’t walking down the road and he pulled over to pick her up. She—”

Michael instantly caught on. He snapped his fingers. “She got out of the car. He’d picked her up somewhere else.”

She nodded. “Bingo.”

“So wait. He let her out of the car, and when she was getting out, he attacked her?”

Rylie shrugged. By now, the others had caught on and were turning to see what the revelation was. Hoskins said, “What’s going on?”

“There are no footprints down the road that suggest the victim hitchhiked to this point. It’s more likely that she was picked up elsewhere, somewhere down the road, and killed here,” Brisbane explained.

Hoskins scratched the side of his face. “Yeah, that makes sense…”

Rylie stared down the highway. “What’s the next exit down that way?”

“That’s Bearmouth. Nothing there but a trailer park. Gas station. It’s pretty quiet.”

That was music to her ears. She headed for her car, calling over her shoulder, “Bris, come on. Let’s go ask around that gas station. There’s a chance that he might have met up with her there.”

CHAPTER SIXTEEN

Half an hour after they left the crime scene, Rylie stood in the break room of a small gas station, staring at a monitor and squeezing her hands into tight fists at her sides.

The technology at this station was a little more modern, so they had all their surveillance video digitized. The cameras were newer, too, and captured several angles, not just in front of the station, but at each pump, too. And the output was as clear as day.

Unfortunately, it didn't tell them anything.

Oh, Eileen Devers had stopped there. That much, they'd easily ascertained. She'd spent quite a long time there, too, and had put on quite a show. She'd gone around delivering brochures to just about everyone she came in contact with. She'd even accosted a vacationing family with three young kids, practically climbing into their minivan despite the wife's obvious annoyance. In the end, though, she'd headed out on foot, toward the interstate.

Alone.

Rylie had hoped that there'd be clear video of the victim accepting a ride with a stranger. Of course, it couldn't be that simple. The clerk hadn't seen anything unusual, either.

"That's great," she muttered to the clerk. "Thanks for your help."

She turned to leave. As she made her way to the front of the store, Michael waved a piece of paper in front of her. "We've got a few cars to keep an eye out for."

He was right. Always looking on the bright side, Bris was. But he was talking about the cars that had parked in the lot at around the same time Eileen Devers was there, and Rylie didn't feel good about any of them. The family with the kids? The teenage girl in the University of Wyoming sweatshirt? And then there'd been the little old lady with a cane.

"Pardon me for my skepticism, Bris. But none of those people looked like the murdering type," she said as she went to the carafe and poured herself an extra-large coffee. She needed it.

She poured a second cup and handed it to him as he looked over the list. "Okay, yeah. They're long shots."

"We don't have license plate numbers either. I don't think I want to waste my breath tracking Granny into Seattle," she muttered as she left a few dollars on the counter.

"Yeah. I guess. But what other ideas do you have?"

"Well, we have a whole pile of cold cases in the back of my truck," she said with a shrug as they went outside and got back into the vehicle. "And from what I remember, there was one about a murder or something in this area. I thought it was a hitchhiker. Sound familiar?"

He shook his head. "From when?"

"It was probably ten, fifteen years ago."

He opened the lid on his coffee and inhaled deeply. "Seriously? Most of the guys on the force wouldn't even remember that. Hoskins would be the only one. Possibly. He's been on the force about fourteen years."

"Well, you can ask him about it, then," she said, heading onto the interstate, in the direction of the Missoula headquarters.

He pulled out his phone, his thumbs working over the display. "I'm texting him right now. But if you're looking through the cold cases for crimes that involve hitchhikers, you're going to get a lot of hits. There's a reason it's illegal."

"Maybe," she said. "But maybe Beaker can come up with a list of cases involving hitchhikers in the area, too?"

He held up a finger. "Say no more. You know he's just dying to help us out. I'll text him, too."

*

An hour later, Rylie sat back in her chair and rubbed her eyes.

Michael had been right. There was no shortage of cases involving hitchhikers in the area. Beaker had sent over a list of them from the past fifteen years. Hoskins hadn't remembered the case Rylie was talking about, but he'd remembered various ones—assaults, robberies, kidnappings—all involving people who'd been walking along the interstate. Rylie felt like she was about to drown in all the information.

"There's too much," she moaned, as Michael sat across from her, chomping on a chocolate frosted muffin. Someone in the office had brought in treats, and of course, he'd been all over that.

He licked the chocolate from his lips and said, "I told you."

She gave him a sour look. "You don't have to rub it in."

He sat up and scooted his chair forward. "Well, what about the case you were thinking about? The murder? There must've been some reason you connected it to this, other than it having a murdered hitchhiker?"

She blew out a long breath. "Yeah. I can't remember. And I can't seem to find it anywhere. It's not with any of the murders. But if I remember right, it might have been more than one. I remember reading that the items were left on the side of the road, close to that Clinton Gas Express."

"More than one murder?" He scrolled through the computer, a doubtful look on his face. "People would remember that."

"Okay, so maybe it wasn't a murder." She leaned forward. "You know, all of the victims so far were in their early twenties. Can you sort that out by the age of the victim? Maybe that will narrow things down a little."

"Of course I can. Contrary to what Beaker thinks, I'm not completely useless around a computer. I mean, I'm not exactly an Excel wizard, but I can…" He stuck out his tongue like a little boy and did a little maneuvering with the mouse, then shouted in triumph. "Voila."

Only one case showed on the screen.

It was the case of a man named Devon Warner.

Her eyes lit up. "That's it. That's the one I was thinking about."

He clicked on it, and it brought them to a link on the case and its files. "Robbery," Michael mused, reading it. "Serial. He had six victims over a period of a few months. But the case is closed. That's why we couldn't find it in the files. How did you know about it?"

"I don't know," she murmured, looking at the face of the man who'd been arrested for the crime. "I guess I must've seen it while we were going over files for the other cases."

Devon Warner. That was his name. His eyes were cold and unfeeling in his mugshot, making him look just like all the other criminals they'd apprehended for terrible crimes. He might have only been arrested for robbery, but she didn't doubt he was capable of much worse.

"Well, it says here that he used to meet up with hitchhikers at gas stations, pick them up, assault and rob them, and leave them on the side of the road. Women and young men under the age of twenty-five. Spent six years in prison for the crimes and was just released a couple years ago."

She scanned through the file. "Where is he now?"

She saw it at the same time he did. Interesting. He was living at an address in Clinton, since his release. "You think he might be our guy?"

Michael shrugged.

The crimes were different. But they were in the same location, and he was in the area. He might have been escalating. It was a possibility.

"All right," she said, scribbling down his address. "Why don't we head over to pay Devon Warner a visit?"

CHAPTER SEVENTEEN

Devon Warner lived in a trailer park like many of the other developments in the area, but this one was much smaller than the other they'd visited. There were only six trailers, situated around a circular dirt drive with a picnic bench in the center of it. As Rylie drove up the straight drive, a woman who was hanging up laundry glared at her from the back of her mobile home. A couple of unseen dogs barked at them.

Michael looked up from the file on Devon Warner. "This guy's got some seriously shady history. He's been arrested for burglary, assault, drugs, you name it."

Rylie hated to celebrate a man's record, but she did an internal fist pump. If they could end this right now, they could be headed back east by nightfall.

But she wasn't getting her hopes up. She'd done that before, with the last lead that had wound up going nowhere.

"This one," Michael said, pointing to the second home in the loop. While the last trailer they'd been to had screamed "bachelor pad," this one had pleasant touches that made it look homey and welcoming. Flowers in window boxes on the façade. A little patio set up with matching furniture. A WELCOME FRIENDS placard near the door. A Chevy Bronco was parked in the driveway, clearly old-model, but free of the layers of dust that seemed to plague most cars. "Doesn't actually look like the home of a murderer, does it?"

Though she'd been thinking the same thing, she wasn't happy to hear him announce it. "Well, if every house announced that a criminal lived inside, we'd be out of a job. You can be neat and a psychopath, too. Just ask Hannibal Lector."

He chuckled as they stepped up to the front door. Before she had a chance to knock, the door swung open, and a man with a drawn, worn face and long, stringy black hair opened it. "No solicitors."

He pointed to a smaller, barely visible sign under the WELCOME FRIENDS sign.

"We're not soliciting," she said, showing her badge. "Devon Warner, we want to ask you a few questions."

His eyes narrowed. "About what?"

"About a series of murders that have been happening on I-86."

His mouth dropped open. "Murders?" He shook his head. "Why are you here? You're not going to try to pin this on me. I'm clean. I'm straight now."

"You are?"

He crossed his arms. "Definitely. I got out of jail. Got myself a job. Went to rehab. I've been off the bottle since I got out. Don't do no drugs, either. You can ask my probation officer."

"You'll give us his name?" Michael asked.

He snarled. "Look. I ain't gotta tell you nothing."

"Will you step outside and talk with us, or can we come in?" Rylie asked, noticing a couple of neighbors looking through the windows.

Warner noticed it, too. "Like I said. I ain't gotta tell you nothing."

"We'd still like to know where you were during these dates," Michael said. "So either you discuss it with us here, or we'll have you arrested and bring you downtown. I promise you, it won't be better there."

The man's face reddened, and he looked like he might blow. As Michael looked down to read the times and dates off his phone, Devon reached behind his back.

"Bris, watch!" Rylie shouted, lunging forward.

Michael was closer, and in the way. He dropped his phone, and in one swift motion, grabbed him easily by the arm and wrenched it behind him, throwing him to the ground. After a few tense seconds of scuffle, he was disarmed. Not that he'd been armed in the first place. When he was down on the ground, Rylie saw what he'd been reaching for—his wallet, which was now open on the steps.

Shoving the man flat against the ground so his cheek kissed the concrete patio, Michael hissed, "So what the hell was that?"

"Fine, fine," Devon breathed out, wincing. "Ask me your questions. I'll answer. Fine. Just let me go."

Michael hefted him up and shoved him down on one of the patio chairs. When he finished breathing hard, he straightened his tie. "All right. So get talking."

Warner looked around sheepishly. "People around here, they know me. Know my past. But ask any of them. We're a family around here. They don't fault me for my past mistakes. And I made peace with the man upstairs. He's the only one I owe anything to, because he gave me back my life. People like you, they just messed it the hell up."

"People like us, you mean—"

"The law. They kept getting in my way. All of you are worth nothin' to me," he growled, leaning over and spitting into the dirt close to Michael's foot.

Michael looked down at the wet circle near his toe and shook his head. "Okay, can you tell me where you were last night? From about midnight to four in the morning?"

He stroked his chin. "Then? Here."

"With anyone?"

He waved a hand. "The only one who can confirm that is my pillow. But my car never left. My neighbors could tell you that."

"What about three nights ago?"

"Here."

Rylie looked around. Likely, he wouldn't have anyone to corroborate his story, since he lived here alone, and most of the crimes had happened late at night. "You ever go down to the I-86 corridor for anything?"

He shook his head. "Not anymore. I stay clear of that place. That highway brought me nothing but trouble." He looked Michael straight in the eye. "I did a lot of things I ain't proud of back then. Because of the drugs, the alcohol. But I'm clean now. I found Jesus."

He reached into the collar of his T-shirt, pulled out a large gold cross, and kissed it.

Michael reached down, grabbed his wallet from the step, and handed it to him. "You have the name of your probation officer?"

He nodded and looked through his wallet. "Kelly. This is what I've got. I was going to show it to you when I was so rudely interrupted," he said, reaching in and pulling out a card. Michael glanced at it and handed it to Rylie. It had a number of dates on it for his appointments with his probation officer. In several years, he hadn't missed a single one.

Rylie handed it back to him, sighed, and looked around at the other trailers. This felt like another waste of time. "Thanks for your time," she said, whirling and heading back to her truck.

"Where now?" Michael asked as they climbed inside.

She really didn't know. It felt like they were at a dead end. Again. "Back to headquarters. Let's see if we can't find something else inside the files to go on."

CHAPTER EIGHTEEN

When they returned to headquarters after another disappointing interview, Rylie noticed someone she never expected to see again standing outside the building.

Cooper Rich, her friend from the Seattle field office.

At first, she thought her mind was playing tricks on her, or that it was just a lookalike. But as she drew nearer, she only confirmed it. There he was, with his curly dark hair, his magazine-worth sense of style, a black suitcase roll tucked at his hip.

What the hell was he doing here? He couldn't have "just been in the neighborhood." There was no way. This place was too remote.

Immediately, her mind went to Bill Matthews, but she shoved that aside as she waved to him from the truck before pulling into a parking space.

"Who's that?" Michael asked, confused. "Friend of yours?"

"Only one of my best friends from Seattle," she said, her veins flooding with excitement. Who cared why he was here? It was good to see him. "He's FBI, too."

Before her partner could say more, she jumped out of the truck and ran to him. "Hey, you," Rich said, smiling at her.

"I couldn't believe my eyes. What brings you all the way out here, Coop?" she said, giving him a hug.

"I had to come out here and visit my favorite FBI agent," he said.

"Yeah, right."

"Okay, okay, I have a case."

She snorted in disbelief. Was he serious? "What case would bring you all the way out here?"

He waved his hand dismissively. "There's a suspect who grew up around here, and they sent me out here to see if I can shake out anything from his past."

She stared up at him. Was he serious? That had Bill Matthews all over it. Getting her dumped from his field office wasn't enough. What was he trying to do to her now? But before she could ask him, she realized he was looking warily over her shoulder. She stepped back and realized Michael Brisbane was standing there.

"Oh, Coop. This is my partner, Michael Brisbane. Michael, this is Cooper Rich."

She expected Michael Brisbane to be his normal, charming self. Instead, he simply reached forward and shook his hand. To her surprise, it was Cooper who spoke first. "Well, well. I never thought our Lone Wolf here would submit to having a partner. You must either have balls of steel, or you're used to letting someone else call all the shots."

Brisbane just stared icily at him. "Something like that."

Rylie laughed and elbowed him. "Stop it! That's bullshit. I don't call all the shots."

He snorted. "Right. Only like ninety-nine percent of them."

She looped her arm through Coop's and led him to the door. Meanwhile, Michael straggled behind, hands in pockets. "Have you been inside? You just get in?"

"Yep. Just came from the airport in my rental car."

"Oh. I'm sure you have a lot to do, but we can at least introduce you around. Michael here—" She looked behind her to find him, now straggling way behind, at the door, staring at the floor. She snapped her fingers, and he looked up. "As I was saying, Michael's from Missoula."

"That so?" Cooper said, the disinterest obvious. "Since I just got in, I want to decompress. You know."

"Oh, sure," she said, sitting him in the conference room. "Want a cup of coffee or something?"

"Yeah, that'd be great."

Michael, who'd been hovering silently in the door, perked up and said, "I'll get it," then disappeared.

She sat across from her friend and smiled at him. "So, this case… weird that you're out here now… I really didn't think I'd ever see you again."

He raised an eyebrow. "You weren't planning to ever come back to Seattle?"

"Not considering how much Bill has it in for me," she said, watching him, waiting for him to tell her the *real* reason he was here. Bill Matthews had sent him to keep tabs on her.

But Coop simply shrugged. "Yeah, well, you know what an idiot he is."

"How are things in Seattle?"

He laughed. "Do you care?"

"Not really. Just being nice." She shrugged off her jacket and said, "Actually, you are the only part of Seattle I care about. So how are you?"

He laughed some more. "Good. Busy. I mean, it sucks in the office without you, calling Bill on his bullshit. He has free rein, now, and he's using it. But other than that, it's good. Bought a house."

"Yeah?" He'd been planning to find a place.

"Yeah. It's nice. Just outside the city."

"Wow, cool. Look at you." He'd never been the most responsible guy, going out to downtown clubs every night, drinking away his paycheck. "Weird. Sounds like Cooper Rich is actually getting his life together."

"I know. Becoming an actual adult."

In her head, she had a flash of what might have been, if she'd just kept her head down and done what Bill Matthews wanted. She and Coop had flirted on and off with the idea of dating, but it had never been the right time. Maybe, if she'd just played along with Bill, the two of them could've been moving into that house, together… Now she had a pathetic bachelor pad in Rapid City that she'd never call a home.

She pushed the thoughts away. "I'm happy for you."

She felt a pang of sadness, not just for him, but more like homesickness for the city. During all the years she'd spent in the Violent Crimes unit in Seattle, she'd thought she was making a life for herself. She'd had a nice apartment, a boyfriend, Joe. She'd thought she'd live her whole life there. But things changed. She and Joe went their separate ways, and after that, things really started to come to a head with Bill Matthews.

He looked over the files scattered on the table. "What are you working on?"

"Oh." She sighed and rolled her eyes, remembering the last suspect they'd pursued, only to wind up at square one again. "A murderer who's been taking victims from I-86. All hitchhikers. Three victims so far."

He shifted the papers around. "Yeah? Any leads?"

"Not many. Everything we've tried to pursue hasn't really led anywhere."

Just then, Michael came into the room with a coffee and a donut on a napkin. He set them in front of Coop, who said, not looking up,

"Thanks, pal," then turned his attention back to Rylie. "So, what? You have any suspects at all?"

She shook her head. "We just got back from the last one, who wound up being a dead end. I'd picked him up from the files of previous cases in the area. He'd committed a lot of robberies along the interstate, been arrested, and just got out of prison. But he checked out. Apparently, he's turned his life around."

"What about video cameras at gas stations and businesses around the highway?"

"We've gotten some video that caught a few of the victims. But it didn't give us any clue to the killer."

He leaned forward over the table. "Tell me about the victims. You said there were three? Female?"

"One was a male," Michael said from the doorway, his voice so low and loud that they both looked up.

"Anything that connects them, besides hitching the interstate?"

"No," Michael said—in fact, he almost snapped it. And was it Rylie, or did he look pissed off? "Nothing."

"The manner of death is the same. Beaten on the head, then strangled."

"Hmm," Coop said, lacing his fingers together under his chin. "So they don't have much in common."

"Yeah, which would make us fairly sure that they're all done by the same guy, but then there are things that make us think it was done by different people altogether."

"Yeah, like what?"

"Well, the tire tracks at two of the scenes are different, and there are no tracks at all at the third one," she said, when suddenly, a bit of an idea popped into her head. "Wait…"

Michael said, "What, Wolf… you thinking of something?"

She nodded. "Maybe that's the reason no one seems to have noticed the car. Maybe it's the same guy, but different vehicles. So someone who has access to different vehicles, like a person who works at a car dealership, or a—"

"A mechanic," Cooper filled in.

"Right," Rylie said.

"We should look into all the auto body shops in the area and—"

"*We* will," Michael said, glaring across the table at the new agent, and an awkward silence ensued.

This time, there was no mistaking it. Michael Brisbane clearly resented Cooper's intrusion.

She needed to defuse the situation. She said, "Thanks, Coop, we'll look into it."

"All right," he said, getting to his feet. "I've got to look into my case, anyway. I'll talk to you when I'm done? Maybe we can go to dinner?"

She smiled. "Sure. Sounds good."

She wasn't sure if they'd actually get to go out to dinner. Because of the nature of their cases, they rarely got to do the social things they planned, even in Seattle. Right now, she had a new lead to pursue. She really hoped this one, unlike the others, would lead somewhere.

CHAPTER NINETEEN

When Cooper Rich stepped out to work on his own case, Rylie was left alone with Michael. She began to pile up the papers. She didn't know what her new partner's problem was, but she didn't want to deal with it. She'd had to spend far too much of her time fighting big men with fragile egos who didn't want their toes stepped on and their glory stolen.

"So what are we doing now?" Michael said, back to his happy-go-lucky tone.

She shrugged, not looking at him. "We're going to get a list of car dealers and mechanics in the area and see what that tells us."

He didn't say anything for a moment. Then he said, "Wait. Are you angry at me?"

"No."

"Yeah, you are. I can tell. You're—"

"Why did you act like such a jerk to Cooper? He's a nice guy, and just trying to help."

He frowned. "Oh, is that what it was? I wasn't. I was—"

"You practically snapped his face off."

He held up a finger. "Okay, if you really want to know. First, he just walks in here like he owns the place. And then he starts coming up with theories on a case he knows nothing about? I'd never pull shit like that. I'd—"

"So you're afraid he might come up with the answer before you do?" She crossed her arms. "Get over it. He's a good guy. Just…"

She stopped. She really hoped he *was* a good guy. If he had something to tell her about Bill Matthews, he would. Wouldn't he?

Michael picked up on her uncertainty. "Just what?"

She waved it off. "Nothing. Can we focus on the case and get that list?"

"You'll be happy to know that while you and your old friend were catching up, I emailed Beaker to send us a list of auto businesses within fifteen miles off the I-86 corridor, marking any close to the areas where the victims were last seen."

She gave him thumbs-up and went to the computer, jiggling the mouse to see if Beaker had delivered yet. "Good job. Here it is."

She opened the spreadsheet he'd sent to find a short list of places. That was the good thing about being in a less populated area of the country—the list was manageable, probably only twenty locations. But that was still too many to visit one by one. "There are three that were within five miles of the victims' last known whereabouts. We should probably start with them."

Michael looked over her shoulder. "Sully's Auto Trader. Sounds shady."

She glared at him. "You can tell? Just by the name?"

"Yep. Look at that. Maxford Sullivan. Maxford? Not only is it a dumb name, it's super shady."

"Oh, that makes a lot of sense."

He let out a huff. "Well, it makes about as much sense as coming into a case without knowing a damn thing about it and offering up theories..."

She pushed away from the computer and faced him. "Really? You're going to go there? What do you have against him? He said it himself. He's here for a totally different case."

"And yet he seems to really like sticking his nose in this one."

She shook her head in disgust. "Are you going to keep doing that?"

"That depends. Are you going to keep defending him?"

She didn't have to deal with this nonsense. She pressed the button to send the list on the computer to the printer. She'd go on this mission without him, and be *just fine.* That's why they called her the Lone Wolf.

When she stood up, before she could stalk out the door, he said, "What, are you guys like, an item?"

She stopped, hardly believing her ears. What difference did it make to him? "Are you kidding me?"

He held up both hands. From the way he physically backed away and hung his head, she didn't have to answer that. He knew he'd gone too far.

She grabbed the list from the printer outside, and when she returned to get her bag and keys, she didn't look at him. She simply grabbed her things and headed for the door.

"Wait. You're not going alone?"

She shot him a look. "I think I'd prefer that, at this point."

"Yeah, maybe," he said, grabbing his things, too, and following her out. "But I'm your partner and this is my case, too."

"Unfortunately," she muttered under her breath. When she got to the door, she stopped and turned. "You can come with me, fine. *If* you promise me one thing."

"What?"

"Cut. The. Bullshit."

"What do you—"

"Whatever that was, in *there*. No one's trying to take over your case. So stop your ego flexing and chill out. Okay?"

He sighed. "Whatever."

Her frown deepened.

"Okay, okay, I'll be good," he said with resolve.

She gave him the evil eye for a little longer, then whirled and went out the door. As soon as they were seated in the truck, she looked at the list. "Sully's it is. Since you have that… you know. *Feeling*."

She had just started to pull out of the parking lot when he pulled his nose out of his cell phone and banged on the console between them.

"Ha!"

She nearly jumped. Did he want her getting into an accident? "What?"

He jabbed a finger at his phone. "Look at this."

"I'm driving," she reminded him.

"Fine, I'll read it to you." He cleared his throat and read, in dramatic fashion, "Bearmouth used car dealer Maxford Sullivan convicted of harassment of several female employees. Right there!"

She snorted. "Wow, you're a real Nostradamus," she muttered. "So is he in jail?"

"Nope. Got out last year after spending three years up north in the county jail. In your face! Told you he was shady!" He pumped his fist.

Rylie rolled her eyes. As interesting as that tidbit of information was, she'd more than had enough of Michael today. What was his problem? Why was he intent on getting on her nerves so much? "Great. Can we just drive there in silence from now on?"

Thankfully, he pressed his lips together and didn't say a word the entire twenty-mile drive.

CHAPTER TWENTY

In the passenger seat of the VW Bug, Lacey Henderson bopped her head to a tune she'd never heard of before. It was probably from some terrible '80s hair band. Her best friend, Iona, had always had the strangest taste in music.

Of course, Iona, in the driver's seat, sung every lyric perfectly. Even though it sounded like screeching to Lacey's untrained ears, leave it to Iona to know every word by heart.

When it was almost over, Lacey turned the volume down. "I've never even heard of that song."

"You've never heard of Sonic Youth? What's wrong with you? How can you not like it?"

"No, I liked it. It was catchy. Just…"

"Not your speed. Got it." Iona winked at her.

Iona knew Lacey well. They'd gone to kindergarten together, and every other grade, and now they were brand new college graduates. In between, they'd rarely spent more than a week apart. So of course, Iona knew better than anyone that Lacey wasn't one to take risks.

Which was why she probably also knew that Lacey was scared to death. She couldn't stop her teeth from chattering in her head, despite the stuffy warmth inside the car. She kept twisting her hands in her lap, as much as she tried to keep them still.

When Iona dropped a hand on Lacey's shoulder, Lacey nearly jumped to the ceiling.

Iona giggled. "Lacey. For the last time. Everything is going to be fine!"

Easy for Iona to say. Iona was fearless. She currently played on the boys hockey team at Montana State University, she'd gone bungee jumping when they visited Costa Rica on spring break, and she didn't give a crap about what anyone else said about her.

Lacey? Not so much.

Lacey had practically been *born* in an unbreakable shell. No matter how many times her best friend tried to nudge her out of it, she stubbornly refused. But when she graduated from college a couple months ago, and the dream job she'd always wanted came up—Yellowstone park ranger—Iona had convinced her to apply. She'd thought nothing would come of it.

But then she got the news. They were offering her an interview. In two days' time, she'd be in front of a selection committee. She'd have to tell them she was the best person for the job.

The thought made Lacey's stomach flip and her mind go blank. Would she really be able to do such a thing without throwing up all over them? She wasn't sure.

She was lucky Iona had suggested driving her, taking a few days' time to check out the scenery, a sort of mini-vacation. Lacey never would've been able to drive. Not as shaky as she felt. "I hope you're right."

"Just be calm, smile, and answer their questions. Remember, you're a good person. And you're totally qualified. You're going to get the job!" Iona said, always her cheerleader.

Lacey rolled the window down a little, dragged in a breath of cool air, and let it out. Feeling better, she said, "It'll be awesome to live up in that area."

"Totally! And I'll come visit you all the time!"

"You will?"

She shrugged. "Sure. Bozeman's great and all, but Yellowstone… that's like total heaven there. You're going to love—"

Suddenly there was a loud pop. A cloud of smoke engulfed them, and Iona swerved. It all happened so fast. One moment, they were cruising down an empty stretch of road, the next the car was making a terrible squealing, crunching noise, tilting to the side as Iona slammed on the brakes and tried to keep the car from careening off the road.

She managed to, swerving back into the lane, but as they slowed, it became pretty obvious that one of the tires had blown out. If the noise of metal grinding against the pavement wasn't enough, the car was slowing on its own, like an animal on its last legs.

"Shit," Iona said, pulling to the side of the road. "This isn't good."

Lacey gave her a look. They'd run into a lot of problems together, but this one barely qualified. "What? You don't know how to change a tire?"

Iona winced. "Oh, I *could*. If I had a spare."

Lacey's jaw dropped. "What? You don't have a spare?"

She shrugged sheepishly. "No. I *do* have one." Before Lacey could relax, she added, "But we were driving on it."

Lacey dragged her hands down her face. "Great! What do we do?" She looked up and down the road. She'd seen a sign for an exit somewhere, but exits in this part of Montana were few and far between.

Lacey grabbed her phone and checked her GPS, but it simply spun. In the upper right-hand corner was the notification no one likes to see: *No service.*

"This isn't good," she mumbled.

Iona smiled. "It's fine. Really. It's not a big deal."

Lacey waved her phone. "We don't have phone service. We haven't seen another car on the road for miles. And you don't think this is a big deal?"

"A car will come along. You'll see," Iona said cheerily, taking off her seatbelt and cutting the ignition. She bounced out of the car, and Lacey joined her at the side of the car where the blowout had occurred, shaking her head. Iona had always been so glass-half-full, and she'd been the opposite. "Look."

Lacey peered at the tire. It'd practically disintegrated to nothing. "Wow."

"Yeah, *wow*. We are so lucky we weren't hurt worse!"

Lacey looked around. *There's still time for that.* It was early afternoon, but that didn't matter. Who knew what kind of wild animals were lurking in the hills surrounding them? Now, the interview she'd been so nervous about was the least of her worries. "Should we try walking to the nearest exit, to find a tow?"

Iona looked up and down the road. "I'm not sure which way is the nearest exit. Maybe we should separate."

"Separate?" Lacey's heart leapt in her throat. "Why?"

"Well, if one of us finds the tow first, we'll just send the truck to pick up the other person. Right?"

Lacey gnawed on her lip. "That sounds dangerous. Maybe I should just stay with the car."

"Don't be silly," Iona said, rubbing her shoulder. "It's only a matter of time before someone comes along. We'll just wave them down."

"That could be dangerous," Lacey said, aghast. "You never know—"

"Look. We've already been through danger. And survived!" She pointed to the broken tire.

Iona's enthusiasm was contagious. Lacey found herself smiling, then laughing as her best friend hip-checked her.

"Seriously, Lace. This is not a big problem. There has to be an exit somewhere nearby. If we get the tow soon and get a new tire put on, we can be on the road tonight. No problem!"

Lacey nodded. "I guess."

They reached into the car and pulled out their purses, then gave each other a hug and started out in the opposite direction. As Lacey walked, she kept looking back at her friend, until she was just a dot on the horizon. Then, a moment later, she disappeared from sight entirely.

Then it was just her and the road. She gulped, her throat feeling dry. She wished she'd brought along some water. It wasn't hot, but it was windy, and the breeze was slapping her cheeks.

I can't believe this is happening, she thought to herself as she walked along the shoulder. The sun overhead blurring the path before her, she felt like she was in the midst of some dystopian novel, the only living soul on Earth. Her breathing quickened. *I bet I miss the interview.*

She sighed. That was Iona. Never thinking, always barreling right ahead, ignoring the grim worries and what-ifs that constantly plagued Lacey. Sometimes, those worries were useful. They stopped you from doing stupid things.

Like breaking down in the middle of nowhere with no spare tire.

It'll be okay, she told herself. After all, Iona always succeeded in everything she set out to do. Sometimes she went a crazy, roundabout way and had oddball adventures, but in the end, she always accomplished her goals. That was why she had a great teaching job waiting for her in Bozeman. She made things happen… just like she would make a tow truck magically appear.

That was why Lacey had agreed so readily to her plan. Had it been anyone else, she would've demanded they stay with the car and wait. But Iona could do no wrong.

As she continued to walk, she saw it, in the distance. An overpass, and a sign. *BEARING BROOK 2 MILES.*

"Yes!" she said aloud, picking up the pace. She could make it two miles. There was probably a gas station there, or someplace she could call a tow.

But it was just then that she heard a sound, at first very quiet, but growing louder and louder. The sound of tires on pavement, behind her.

She whirled to see a sedan coming toward her.

Gnawing on her lip, Lacey considered. She'd told Iona that hitchhiking was dangerous. But if the person pulled over, maybe she'd be spared the two-mile walk and get to civilization sooner. Or maybe Iona was already inside, and had summoned help.

But the car didn't slow as it approached her. No, it kept going at the speed limit, eighty miles per hour. Although she only saw a quick silhouette of the driver, a man wearing dark sunglasses, he didn't even appear to turn her way.

The face in the back window passed by in a split second's blur, but it imprinted itself in Lacey's mind. She didn't register that it belonged to anyone she knew. The only thing she noticed was that there was panic in its features.

Just when it passed by, just when Lacey's spirits were about to fall, she noticed something else. Curly, dirty blonde hair, darker at the roots, in the back window.

Lacey knew that hair.

It was Iona. She was sure of it.

But why on Earth had she just kept going?

And… wait. Was that a cop car? It was a plain white sedan. It kind of looked like one. But it didn't have any markings on the doors. And if so, why had he left her behind? Was he taking Iona to jail?

Lacey stared for a moment, sure that they'd made a mistake and would soon return to pick her up. But it never happened. She took a step, and then another, thinking about that cop car, tossing so many questions around in her mind. She continued walking for the exit, faster and faster, until she was running, the interview now further than ever from her mind. The tow truck was, too.

Now, she was worried about her friend. The first call she would make would be to the police.

CHAPTER TWENTY ONE

As Rylie pulled off the highway, onto the road that Sully's Auto Trader was supposedly located on, she had a bit of a déjà vu to Story Creek. A lot of these towns in the middle of nowhere were like that—a single gas station, a few no-tell motels, and miles and miles of wilderness in almost every direction you looked.

This exit didn't even have a gas station. It was that remote. It led her to wonder exactly why anyone would want to start a business here. It wasn't like there was a healthy clientele around. As far as she could see, there was *no one* around.

"Bet this place has killer night life," Michael quipped, reading her mind as he fished in the bottom of a potato chip bag for the last chip.

She tapped the GPS. "Are we sure this is right? It says it should be right up here..."

She squinted. Sure enough, they neared a rusty fence. Inside the fence, which looked like something that was meant to keep people in rather than keep them out, were a number of rusty clunkers on their last legs. It was like an assembly of the ugliest vehicles that had ever been on the road.

"Wow, that's—yikes," she said, momentarily forgetting that she was supposed to be mad at Michael. "I'm almost afraid to turn in."

"You? Afraid? Ha."

"I didn't say I wasn't going to do it," she said, finding the opening in the fence and turning in. They were greeted by a one-floor, white-walled building that was so small, it seemed to be hiding among some of the larger trucks and piles of rusty junk parts in the lot. The entire place looked like it was booby-trapped to give people tetanus. Rylie had a hard time deciding where, among all the junk, to park.

Eventually, afraid to get something in her tire, she cut the engine right where she idled, directly in front of the building. As she stepped out, a man in a red visor, long denim shorts, and sports socks up to his hairy knees stepped out, jogging to them. He was probably mid-forties, and in good shape.

"Hey, folks," he said cheerfully, giving them a wave. "Looking for a new set of wheels?"

She flashed her credentials. "Maxford Sullivan?"

His cheesy smile fell apart instantly, to a deep scowl. "What is this about?"

Michael said, "We'd like to question you in regards to some women and—"

"No, no, no." He waved his hands in front of him, like an umpire declaring a runner safe on base. "I already said my piece about those girls. You're not going to pin anything else on me. If you think you're going to get one more word out of me, trust me, you won't, not without my lawyer present."

He turned to go back into the office.

Rylie said, "This isn't about the harassment."

He stopped. "What is it?"

"Some hitchhikers are dead. Three, to be exact. Do you know anything about that?"

"Dead?" The word was almost a whisper. "Around here? Are you serious?"

She nodded. "Very close to here."

"Huh, yeah," he said pensively, shaking his head. "I thought I heard something about that on the radio. But I thought it was in Denver. Or in one of the bigger cities. Not around here…"

"No. The last victim was found only a few miles from here. And due to your past…"

His face dropped to a scowl and he scoffed. "Right. Due to my past, I was the first suspect on your list. All right, I get it. Makes a lot of sense. Giving girls a little red-carpet treatment is just the same as bludgeoning them to death."

Michael raised an eyebrow. "We didn't actually say how they died."

"Geez." He scrubbed his hands through his hair. "The radio did! That's how I knew about it."

If the radio had been saying that, it was wrong. They'd been strangled, too. As Rylie eyed him, trying to decide whether he was telling the truth, he exploded again.

"Look, yeah. I might have gotten a little cozy with a few of my employees. And then later on, they complain it's harassment." He looked at Michael. "You know how those crazy bitches roll, don't you?"

If he was looking to Michael for help, he didn't get it. Michael shook his head.

But Sully kept on going, sounding more and more like someone Rylie would've loved to punch. "And yeah, okay, a few girls came in for test drives and I might have gotten a little handsy with them, but that's because I'm Italian. I like to touch people. I'm touchy-feely. But in a nice way. There's nothing wrong with touching."

"I think there's *something* wrong with touching," Michael said. "Especially if the woman's not into it. And I'm wagering since you've had more than one misunderstanding with women, it might have something to do with you. What do you think, pal?"

Sully frowned. "Yeah. All right. I might need to rein it in. I told the judge that. I'll be better from now on. And I have been. I'm married. Got two kids. I'm trying to play the straight and narrow, be someone they can look up to. But I don't know anything about any murdered hitchhikers."

"Tell me, then," Rylie said. "Where were you last night?"

"Last night? I was home. All night. With my buddies. We have poker night every week. They didn't leave here until after three. I live up in Missoula." He nodded eagerly and reached into his pocket. "If you want them to tell you, I can get one of them on the phone…"

"That's not necessary," she said, looking over at Michael. If he had an alibi, that meant that Shady Sully wasn't their guy either. Rylie paced around, taking deep breaths of dusty air and looking at the cars. If she were a hitchhiker, would she set foot in a hunk of junk like these? No. They all looked like they belonged to serial killers. Rusty clunkers, the lot of them. If she was looking for a ride, no matter how desperate she was, she'd probably have passed up all of these cars, if they stopped for her.

And if she wouldn't get in a car like these, there was a good chance none of the others would have, either.

She sighed, trying to decide where this left them.

Nowhere. They had a few more car places on their list, but this one had been, by far, their most promising option. "I think we should go," Rylie mumbled, heading for her car. They'd driven all the way out here, wasting time… for what? The killer could be out right now, chasing down his next victim. Another dead body tonight. And here they were, at another dead end. It wouldn't technically be her fault if another person died… but Rylie didn't care about technicalities. She'd feel responsible, nonetheless.

Michael continued to ask a few questions about whether he knew of any other suspicious activity in the area, and she listened half-heartedly, thinking about the other names on the list. If they were going to track those places down by close of business, they needed to get on the road soon. “Michael,” she said gently. “We should go.”

He thanked Sully, just as cordially as he did anyone, and they climbed into the truck. “Well, another roadblock.”

“Yeah.” She looked at the time on the dashboard clock. It was after three. “Let’s hurry and try to get over to these other places on the list. If that doesn’t turn something up…”

She didn’t finish, because she didn’t even want to think about it, but it still hung heavily in her mind.

If it didn’t turn something up, they were right back at square one, with lives at stake, and a killer on the loose.

CHAPTER TWENTY TWO

As Rylie drove them back to headquarters, her phone, sitting in the cup holder, lit up with a text. She was just about to glance at it when Michael let out a grunt. "You got a dinner invitation."

Glaring at him, she picked it up. Sure enough, it was from Cooper. *If you're not busy, let's do dinner.*

She was a little annoyed at her partner for reading her texts, but even more annoyed that the tone of his voice seemed to indicate he believed in something that wasn't there between Cooper and her.

That again? Sure, they'd flirted, but so had she and Michael. It didn't mean anything. And she was tired of dealing with it. She needed to nip it in the bud.

"Bris, if I was interested in going out to dinner with Coop, which I'm not, because I'm in the middle of a case—you would be invited, too."

"Of course you're not interested in eating," he grumbled. "But does Coop know you aren't interested in him?"

She glanced over at him as headquarters came into view. "What is that supposed to mean?"

He shrugged. "Just that he looks like he's into you."

Her eyes narrowed. "He's not. And what does any of this have to do with you, anyway? Seriously, can you stop harping on it?"

He sighed. "Nothing. I was just teasing you."

It hadn't *sounded* like teasing. Teasing was fun. There hadn't been anything playful about his tone. It sounded like he was going straight for the jugular. "Well, if that's what you call teasing, you can stop."

He snorted and turned his attention to the front of headquarters. "Speaking of loverboy…"

"Bris!" Before she could lay into him for being an utter jerk, she noticed what he was talking about. Cooper Rich was sitting on the steps outside headquarters, his phone in his hands, busily texting away. Was he waiting for her?

Something tickled in the back of her mind. *You know there's no case. Bill Matthews sent him to get dirt on you.*

That was ridiculous, though. Wasn't it?

She'd have to ask him, eventually. When they were alone. She certainly couldn't talk to him with Michael around, making all these ridiculous assumptions about her love life like some bratty younger brother.

She jumped out of the truck and as she was walking toward him, she shouted, "Coop! What did you do, get done with your case early?"

He had a peculiar look on his face. "You get my text?"

Glancing at Michael, she said, "Yeah, but I'll have to take a raincheck on dinner, unfortunately. I'm too in the middle of this case to—"

"Not that one. The last one I sent."

She pulled out her phone and read: *Police just brought in a girl that might have info on your case.*

Her eyes widened as she reached the front steps and started to jog up them. "Where is she?"

"Inside."

"What's going on?" Michael said, following close behind her.

She handed him the phone.

"Oh, shit," he said, reading it.

The moment they stepped in, they saw her, sitting on one of the chairs in the lobby. She wasn't hard to spot, because every uniformed officer in the area was hovering around her in a semicircle. Rylie nudged them away, trying to give the girl breathing room, and they eventually parted to let her through.

"Guys, back off. Give her room," she said as she made it to the center of the fray. There was a girl with a dark pixie cut, jeans, and a pale face streaked with tears. She was breathing hard, hysterical.

At that moment, she had a flashback. Déjà vu. She tried to push it off, but it gripped her hard. Rylie, sitting in the police station, while all the adults in uniform swarmed around her. She'd been only nine, and awkward, in her bloody, dirty jeans and messy pixie cut that her mother had insisted she get, *because it'll be so much easier to handle!* She'd hated that haircut, thought it made her look like a boy. But right then, she'd been scared to death, so scared, she couldn't even force a single word out of her mouth.

It was only after a female officer had spoken to her, calmly and soothingly, that she began to open up.

So Rylie did the same. She crouched in front of the young girl, who couldn't have been more than twenty-one, and spoke in the same tone that female officer had used with her that day. "Okay, it's all right. You're safe. Hi. I'm Agent Rylie Wolf from the FBI. And you are?"

"L—L—L—" the girl stammered, then covered her face and started to sob.

Hoskins leaned in. "That's Lac—"

She held up a hand. "Can you give us some space?" She was already in a fragile state, and all this attention was probably making things worse and less comfortable for her. What she needed was some of her partner's soft touch. She wasn't sure she could do that on her own. "Actually, why don't we go into the back conference room? It'll be more private there."

The girl nodded and they walked together to the back room. As she ushered the poor girl into the room, Michael appeared with a bottle of water for her. Together, they could get her to calm down.

"All right," Rylie said, sitting beside her, so that she wouldn't feel like this was an interrogation. "It's just the three of us. Why don't you start by telling us your name?"

"Lacey," she said, wiping the tears from her eyes. "Lacey Henderson."

"Good," Rylie said encouragingly. "Why don't you tell me what's going on? What brings you in here?"

She sniffed. Michael handed her a tissue, which she took, dabbing at her eyes. "My friend and I were going to Yellowstone. I have a job interview there tomorrow, for park ranger."

"Okay. What's your friend's name?"

"Iona." She reached into her purse and pulled out her phone, where she scrolled through and presented them with a photograph of a tiny girl with more curly, dirty blonde hair than body. She was definitely pretty. In the photograph, she and Lacey were wearing matching parkas, standing together atop a hill, overlooking a snowy valley below.

"All right. So you were headed up to Yellowstone. What happened?"

"It was terrible. Her car broke down on the interstate. Our tire blew out, and she didn't have a spare. In the middle of nowhere. There was no one around to flag down." She swallowed. "We didn't know where we were. There was no phone service out there to call a tow. At first, I thought we were screwed. But she never worries. She had the idea that we should split up and go separate directions to find help, because all those exits down there don't have much. That way, the first person to find help would just send a car to pick up the other one. And… and…"

At that, a memory must've gripped her, because she buried her face in her hands and began to sob. "It's so terrible," she wailed. "You have to find my friend."

"We're going to do our best. But we need more information." Rylie glanced at Michael. Iona clearly wasn't there with them. Had she been taken by this madman? In broad daylight? While they were wasting time talking to Shady Sully?

"Where's your friend?" Michael asked. "Did she disappear?"

She kept sobbing.

"Lacey, listen to me," Rylie said, leaning in. "We want to help you, but you have to tell us what happened to your friend. Where's Iona now?"

"Gone," she sobbed. "She's gone…"

"You didn't see her again, after you two separated on the highway?" Michael asked.

"No, no." She dragged her hands down her face. "I saw her. That's the thing. That's when I knew something was really wrong. She was in the back of a white sedan, and I think she was scared. I think someone kidnapped her."

A white sedan. Rylie straightened. "When did you see this?"

"While I was walking. At first, I thought she'd found help, and she'd stop. But the driver didn't slow. He just kept going as if I weren't even there!" She wiped at her nose, then grabbed the neck of the water bottle and unscrewed the cap. "And I thought they'd come back, but they didn't. And the more time that passed, the more I knew something was wrong. So I ran all the way to the next exit, found a phone, and called the police."

"Did you see the man in the driver's seat of the car?" Michael asked.

She nodded. "Barely. A little. It all happened so fast. He was wearing mirrored sunglasses. And he was looking straight ahead." She shuddered. "He looked really mean. I just can't imagine Iona—Iona…"

She covered her face with her hands again.

"Are you sure it was Iona?" Rylie asked.

"Definitely. Well, at first I wasn't sure. I only saw the face for a split second, and it didn't look like her. She looked scared, and Iona never looked scared. But then I saw her hair in the back window, and I knew it was her."

"And what was she doing?"

"She was in the back seat. And she looked at me. There was panic on her face, I think." She swallowed hard. "It was weird, because Iona didn't panic. She prided herself on having everything under control. But there was definite worry in her eyes. Like she was begging me to help her."

Michael looked at the map on the wall. "Where on I-86 was this?"

She shook her head. "I—I don't—"

"Can you point it out to me on the map?"

The girl looked at it, then stood up and walked over to it. After a few moments, she said, "This was the exit. Our tire blew out at around here. I remember the milepost as I was walking was 91."

Rylie got up and looked at it. Clinton. Just around where the other bodies had been found.

"This sedan… can you describe it for us? Did it have any distinguishing characteristics?" Rylie asked. "Maybe a model? Part of a license plate? Was it old or new? Have anything hanging from the mirror?"

She shook her head. "It was mid-sized. Pretty new, I guess. And… it kind of looked like the same model of the guy who lives across the street from me in Bozeman." She gnawed on her lip. "But he's a police officer, so minus all the markings on the doors."

Rylie was about to ask another question, but Lacey let out a little cry.

"It just doesn't make any sense. You don't know Iona. She could be reckless, but she was also a fighter. She wouldn't just let a guy kidnap her. She'd fight him to the death. And in the back of that car, she looked panicked, which was weird, but almost… I don't know how to say it. Resigned. Like she accepted it. And that was even weirder."

Rylie shook her head. "I don't understand…"

"I don't understand it either!" She threw her hands up. "I don't know why she was like that, but all I know is something was wrong! She was in trouble. You've got to find her. She's my best friend, and we were only out here because she agreed to take me up to this interview, since I was too nervous. And now…"

Rylie patted her back. "It's all right. We're going to do everything possible to help find your sister."

Michael stiffened, and she wasn't sure why. When she looked up at him, he mouthed, *Her friend. Not her sister.*

Rylie swallowed. "Of course, I mean your friend." She fought the blush on her cheeks, knowing that Michael was staring at her curiously, likely able to see everything going on in her mind. "Why don't we get you something to eat and bring you someplace quiet? Is there someone we can call to come here for you?"

The girl nodded. "My parents live in Bozeman."

"All right. Great. We'll call them and see if they can't come here to be with you right now. Is that okay?"

She sniffled and sat down in a chair. "Yes. Thank you."

"All right. Just wait here one moment, and I'll be back in a little bit, okay?" She patted her knee and headed for the door.

Outside, Michael said, "Who knew you had all that compassion in that hard heart of yours?"

She waved him away, not meeting his eyes. Maybe he wasn't saying it, but he must've known that she'd been thinking of her own harrowing situation, decades before, while she interviewed that girl. "She was obviously scared to death," she mumbled dismissively, turning to the important business at hand. "We have to get on that white sedan. See if we can find the girl. Get an APB out."

"Done. And?"

"I think we need to go out to where her car broke down and check things out. See if we can't find this white sedan ourselves."

He followed close on her heels to the front counter, where she stopped to give the officer there directions on what to do with poor Lacey.

When she finished, she looked at Michael, who was just hanging around, twiddling his thumbs. "Did you inform them to put out the APB?"

He nodded. "I told you. Already done."

"Good." She turned and headed out the door. "Because the sooner we find that white sedan, the sooner—"

She stopped when she realized there were a half-dozen white sedans in the lot, lined up together, all matching the description Lacey had given them. Unmarked police cars, so that officers could more easily make traffic stops without alerting speeding drivers to their presence.

A thought occurred to her, just as Cooper emerged from his rental car and jogged over to them. "No dinner, then?"

Michael glared at him. "We have other things to do, so—"

"No, no dinner," she mumbled, almost to herself, the thought taking root in her mind.

"You okay?" Both Cooper and Brisbane said to her, at the exact same time.

She stepped back, feeling another flash of déjà vu, like she was being cornered. "Yeah, I'm fine. I was just thinking. The white sedan…"

They followed her line of sight to the other sedans parked across the lot. "What about it?" Brisbane said.

"What if it's a cop?"

They both said the same thing, in perfect sync: "What?"

The thought grew in her mind, supporting facts coming back to her. "It makes sense. Lacey said her friend would've fought a kidnapper. Why would she go willingly? Why would she be sitting in the back of the car and not the trunk? Maybe she thought she was being arrested by the police?"

Michael snapped his fingers. "Make sense." He went back and opened the doors to headquarters. "I'll ask and see if we can get a list of unmarked police cars in the area and who they belong to."

He went inside, leaving her alone with Cooper. When she hurried to her truck, he followed. She looked back. "Don't you have to do some work on your case?"

"All done for the day. I'll come with?"

She stiffened at the thought. One partner was more than enough. "Thanks, but Michael and I have it."

"Yeah, but maybe I can help. I can—"

"Coop. Why are you here?" she blurted, fixing him with a hard stare.

"What do you mean? I told you—"

"Admit it. You're spying on me. For Bill. Admit it. He moved me out to this godforsaken place, but that's not enough, is it? Is he looking for something more to report to his dad so that he can finally rid the force of me for good?"

Cooper Rich looked away. "No… it's not."

She crossed her arms. "Then what is it?"

"The truth is," he said, still looking at a place over her head. "The truth is… I asked for this assignment. Because I wanted to see you. I missed you, Rylie."

She never thought she'd be the one to turn into a puddle of goo at the words of a man. Sad movies and songs didn't get her all maudlin, like they did other girls. Romance made her want to roll her eyes. But sure enough, she felt her face heating. An unwanted smile crept on her lips, as much as she tried to stop it. "Really?"

He nodded. "That's why I was hoping we could go to dinner…"

She smiled. "That's nice. But you know I can't. I have this case. Maybe… how long will you be in town?"

"A few more days," he said, touching her arm. "It's okay. I know you don't need me for this. I just wanted to spend time with you."

Out of the corner of her eye, she saw movement and turned to find Michael, staring at her. "We ready?" he ground out, his voice low.

Had he heard any of that? She nodded and took a step away from Cooper. "Yeah."

Cooper Rich said, "Yeah. You go on. And I'll take a raincheck on that dinner."

Michael had definitely heard that. There was no use denying it. "Yeah, sure," she said casually, opening the driver's side door. "Some other time."

When she pulled out of the parking spot, Michael sat there, not saying a word. The look on his face said everything she needed to know. He was angry again. And why? She'd told Cooper to get lost. He should've been happy about that.

"Let's concentrate on this police car," she mumbled to him as she pulled out onto the highway. "The police are looking into it?"

He nodded. "Let's get back to the broken-down car and see if we can find any clues out there as to where they went."

CHAPTER TWENTY THREE

This was too good to pass up.

The man had just finished with the other girl. She'd been a pain in the ass. Mouthy, screaming at the top of her lungs when she knew she was in danger. She thought she was so damn smart. That she could outwit him.

But she'd been wrong. They'd all been wrong.

She had fought him more than he'd liked—he had the bruises on his chest and a bloody nose to show for it. She was definitely frisky. After he'd squeezed the life out of her, he'd gone back to his car, thinking, *That's it. I'm done. I'll lie low and stay out of sight, and eventually, the police will forget about me.*

But then he'd seen her, walking along the side of the road.

It was like a buffet of all his favorite things, laid out there, just to tempt him. Long, brownish hair. Skinny limbs. Underdressed and limping slightly, probably because she'd been walking much longer than she'd expected to. She was dragging a wheeled suitcase behind her, one with flowers all over it, and her flannel shirt hung loosely, sadly, from her frame.

She was playing desperate.

But he knew what she really was. Evil.

As evil as the hitchhiker who'd beaten Eloise.

He slowed slightly as she came into view, considering. His hands were still shaking from the last one. He wiped at his nose. It had stopped bleeding. The adrenaline from the last one was already wearing off. It was almost as if he could hear Eloise whispering to him. *Just this last one. Then you can rest.*

This one. He could do one more. Then he would lie low.

He pressed on his brakes, then slowed and pulled over to the shoulder, in front of the woman. The more he watched her, the more he knew it was good that he'd stopped. She hesitated there, behind him, as if wondering if she was in trouble. They always did.

He opened the door and looked around. Again, the highway was empty. People might pass by, but they wouldn't see anything. Just a cop talking to a hitchhiker. No problem.

"Howdy," he said as he stepped out of the car, with a half-circle wave. "You headed somewhere?"

She nodded. "Eh… I do not know."

Ah. Her English was heavily accented. She was probably one of those exchange students. How she'd gotten way out here, he didn't know. But it was good that she was far from home. No one would worry about her until it was far too late.

"Well, you're headed toward Missoula. Is that—"

"*Sí!* That is it. Missoula."

"That's not far. Where you coming from?"

"I am a student. From Spain. I hike."

"You supposed to be with a host family?"

She frowned. "My host family no good. I leave. Tell them I have new home in Missoula." She said the word with difficulty. "They want to drive me, but the father, he has hands. All over. I say no. I go myself."

"Ah. Unfortunately, hitchhiking is not legal here," he explained. When she looked at him in confusion, he stuck his thumb out and shook his head. "Not allowed."

Her eyes widened. "Oh! No. I don't beg for rides. I go myself. It okay?"

He shook his head. "No, we don't allow people to walk along the interstates unless their car broke down. And I'm a police officer." He motioned to the badge on his chest. "It's my job to crack down on these infractions. So unfortunately, if you don't have a vehicle…"

Her brow wrinkled, and for a moment, he thought she might cry.

"But don't worry. Since it's your first offense, I'll let you off with a warning," he said, reaching into his utility belt and pulling out his pad of citations.

"A warning?"

"Yes, you won't be charged with a crime," he explained.

"Oh, *gracias*." She smiled. "I do not want to cause no trouble."

He scribbled something, but then shook his head. "You know what, forget it. Tell you what. We can keep it just between you and me. You're new to the country, and have had a hard time. How could you have known?"

She nodded. "*Sí*. I am a good girl. "

"Look. How about this." He shoved his pad into his belt. "I was headed up to the city myself. I can drive you up to the house if you give me directions."

She glanced at his badge. Then she nodded. "Oh, *gracias*. Thank you. Very kind."

He reached down and grabbed her bag. Then he walked her to the back of his car, peering in before he did to make sure that other girl hadn't left anything behind. She hadn't. It was clean. She let the girl in and said, "What's your name?"

"Marta."

"Hi, Marta. I'm Officer Bixby." He smiled and pointed to the brass nameplate.

She smiled back.

"One moment, let me put your bag in the trunk, and then we'll be off."

He closed the door, then went to the trunk. Inside were the bags of the other women. Though he switched cars, he kept the bags with him. He'd get rid of them eventually, but right now, it gave him a little thrill to drive around with them. He'd always thrived upon that kind of danger, on the excitement of almost getting caught. Seeing them there gave him an overwhelming sense of satisfaction. A collection, and an impressive one, at that.

He slammed the trunk and strode confidently to the driver's seat, slid in, and pressed the button to lock the doors. Then he smiled into the back seat. "All right. Just a moment and we'll be on our way."

He pulled off the shoulder, driving north, toward Missoula. As he did, he grinned. This was working out so perfectly. Two woman in one day. Luck was definitely on his side.

Now, all he had to do was find a place to pull over before Missoula, and commence with the fun stuff.

"You are no policeman," she said suddenly.

He stiffened and glanced in his rearview mirror. "I'm sorry?"

She laughed. "In my country, we have many like you. You play games. Especially with young girls you think are stupid. But I am not stupid, sir. I know very much. And I am not an exchange student."

What the hell? He looked down and noticed the pistol in her hand.

Aimed straight at the side of his head.

No. This was bullshit. He was the one who was supposed to be making the plays. Not this stupid, naïve girl.

"Who the hell are you? What the hell do you want?" he snarled.

She grinned. "Let's just say I shouldn't be in the country. I'm making a special delivery, and you're helping me. But you're also going to give me all of your money, too." She held out a hand. "Your wallet, *por favor*."

Like hell.

He'd rather die than let another woman get the best of him.

In a split second, he made the decision.

With all his might, he turned the steering wheel hard to the right, heading off for the shoulder. While she was off-balance, losing her aim, he reached behind her and snatched at the gun.

She let out a shriek as his fingers wrapped around the barrel and he pulled it toward her. She pulled the trigger, but nothing happened. It wasn't loaded.

Stupid woman, he thought, flinging the gun into the passenger foot well and turning to look forward. But before he could right the car onto the highway, she unleashed a torrent of curses at him and flung herself over the console at him. The force of her body sent the wheel spinning out of control, and the car careening toward the grassy median.

"Bitch!" he shouted, grabbing behind him, his fingers tangling in her long hair. He tried to rip his hands out, to grasp the wheel, but he was hopelessly trapped. She threw herself on him, scraping her long fingernails down the side of his face. "Bitch, let go!"

It was too late. They hit the edge of the asphalt, climbed up a short embankment, and then they were airborne for a time, the ground rising up to meet the windshield so fast that he didn't even have time to brace himself. The sound of squealing tires and crunching metal was eardrum-bursting as they hit the ground and rolled up against the guardrail.

Thank goodness for his seatbelt. It cushioned him as his body was flung forward, only to be wrenched back against the hard seat.

When all fell quiet and still again, and he pulled open his eyes, wishing to see the lifeless body of the girl, wedged within a spiderweb of blood-spattered broken glass of the windshield.

But the windshield was perfectly intact. Despite all it had gone through, the car was still on the road, and seemed to be in remarkably good condition. Before he could sigh with relief, he remembered.

The girl. That bitch who'd nearly killed them both.

He scrambled to remove his seatbelt, then twisted to see where she was.

The back seat of his car was empty, the door hanging open. He felt for his pocket, for his wallet. It was still there, thank god, but the girl? She'd run off.

Hardly able to believe it, he reached for the door and pulled himself out. After all that spinning, he was dizzy and disoriented, tripping over the uneven ground as he tried to find his footing. When he did, he looked everywhere. There were a few small footprints on the shoulder, heading north. He followed them, coughing and choking on blood and dust, but when he reached their end, he scanned as far as he could in all directions, and saw nothing.

The woman had disappeared.

Muttering a curse under his breath, he went back to the car and slid inside. He turned the ignition, and miraculously, it started up. Then he rolled out onto the interstate, his head throbbing and his vision double.

He'd get that woman. If it was the last thing he did, he'd make sure she paid.

CHAPTER TWENTY FOUR

Rylie glanced over at Michael, in the front passenger's seat. For the first time since she'd met him, he'd barely said a word. Usually, she'd have been happy to be blessed with quiet. But for some reason, she couldn't help being annoyed at him.

"What is your problem?" she said when they were still a few miles out from the scene of the young women's broken-down car.

He shrugged. "Nothing."

She glared at him. Could he possibly act any more like a sulky teenager? "I think there's something wrong."

"No. I just don't like anyone stepping in on my territory. That's all."

"I agree. Which is why I told Rich we didn't need his help when he asked to come. I already have to deal with you. I don't want or need another partner."

The corner of his mouth lifted into a smile, and he chuckled. "Yeah. I've noticed that about you. But you have to know, that guy is into you."

She wouldn't have thought so before. In fact, she would've adamantly denied it. But then she thought about what he'd told her, while looking into her eyes. *I asked for this assignment. Because I wanted to see you. I missed you, Rylie. I just want to spend time with you.*

It'd hit her like a ton of bricks. How come he'd never said those words when she was in Seattle? Sure, they'd both been dating other people, but now they lived thousands of miles away from each other. Talk about complicated.

Rylie didn't want to think about it. She had a case to solve. And yet, every so often, it trickled in, making her warm and tingly all over.

Shoving those feelings away, she said, "Maybe. But I'm not interested in that. He and I are friends, and it's good to see him, but that's it."

Michael just shrugged, as if he wasn't interested. But if he wasn't interested, why would he even bring it up? Was he trying to rile her up again? They did that a lot, poking fun at one another, trying to get a rise out of each other. If so, she wished he would stop. She pressed on the gas, urging the car to go faster.

Luckily, they found the old VW Bug parked on the side of the road, exactly where Lacey had said it would be. There was also a cop car there, and a tow truck.

As Rylie prepared to step out, Michael's phone rang. "Hoskins," he murmured, picking it up.

She wished she'd been on the receiving end of that call. Michael had left a message with Hoskins a few minutes before, to tell Hoskins the law enforcement idea and ask if there were any cops on the force with questionable behavior. Now, he was calling back.

"Hey, Hos," Michael spoke into the receiver. "Yeah. Yeah. Got it."

Rylie turned to Michael as he spoke, eager to hear more. "Can you put it on speaker?"

He turned away from her and put a finger in his ear. "Okay. Yeah."

Really? So he was going to exclude her? "Hello! What is he saying?"

"Hmm. Yeah. One second." He finally pulled his mouth from the receiver and covered it, saying to her, "He says he doesn't know of anyone on the force who'd do something like that."

She rolled her eyes. "Of course he'd say that!"

She didn't blame Hoskins for doing that, saying that they all had impeccable records. Officers stood up for one another. But Rylie knew that wasn't true. She'd never speak ill of anyone on her force, but all of them had their quirks. Some of them might have even been involved in illegal things.

Michael said back into the phone, "Yeah. Right." He chuckled.

"Let me speak to him," she said, reaching for the phone. On the second try, she managed to grab it from Michael's hands. "Hey!" he shouted, reaching for it back.

She nudged him off and put the phone to her ear. "Hey. Hoskins? It's Wolf."

"Uh… Wolf. How you doing?" He sounded uncertain.

"Yeah, great. I get that you can't imagine anyone on the force committing murder. We're not asking you to think of that. Just… can you think of anyone on the force who might often patrol the area in the unmarked police cars? Who has a history of going against authority? Who might be a little bit of a loose cannon at times?"

He paused. "When you put it that way…yeah. A name does spring to mind."

Now it was Michael's turn to be curious. "What's he saying?" he asked in the background, but she just waved him off. She sure as hell wasn't going to put it on speaker when he hadn't done the same for her.

"Okay, do you know where we can find him?"

"You didn't hear it from me. But the chief is constantly getting on a trooper named Rene Scott. He's been on the force for a lot longer than most people, and so he doesn't respect authority. He's gotten written up a few times for turning his scanner or dash camera off, not being where he's supposed to be, that kind of thing. But he's a nice guy, so—"

"I get it. Thanks. Do you know where he might be right now?"

"He's on shift. I can radio him. One second."

"Yes, please." She smiled and looked over at Michael, who was glaring at her. "Rene Scott. Has a bit of an unreliable history. Hoskins is trying to locate him for us."

Michael crossed his arms. "Uh-huh."

This time, when Hoskins came back, she put him on speaker just as he was saying, "Interestingly enough, he's not answering. So I pinged the GPS in his police car and he's at the Grand Fork Rest Stop."

Michael nodded. "That's about ten miles up the road from here, on the interstate."

She blinked. "Really?"

"Yeah."

Her heart sped up. Rene Scott was in the area. If he'd kidnapped that friend of Lacey Henderson's, maybe he was holding her there right now. Maybe they could intercept it.

The abandoned car would have to wait. She pulled her seatbelt back on. "We're on our way, Hos," she said, already pulling out, hoping against hope that the killer's latest victim was still alive.

*

Rylie was pushing one hundred miles per hour when the first signs for the Grand Fork Rest Stop came into view, right outside the city limits of Missoula.

She floored the gas pedal the whole way, even when taking the long ramp beyond the trees that separated the stop from the highway. A couple of trucks were parked on the straightaway, but other than that, the vast lot was empty. The stop offered no gas, no facilities except for a small building with restrooms and vending machines.

"Maybe he's already left," Michael said, scanning the area. The sun was setting, now, the trees painting long shadows everywhere, making it difficult to see. He grabbed his phone. "I'll call Hos and ask him to track his GPS. Maybe he moved on."

"No! Wait! There!" Rylie blurted as they passed the bank of restrooms. On the other side, parked among the bushes, hidden from the street and most of the parking lot, was a white sedan. Her heart thundered in her chest. From where she was, she could see the silhouette of a form moving beyond the tinted windows.

She barely came to a complete stop before she fumbled to get loose of the seatbelt and throw open the door. Reaching for the gun at her hip, she crossed the lot and reached the sidewalk, Michael close behind her. As she moved forward, she saw more movement in the back seat. The front seat, though, was empty.

"Someone's in there," Michael whispered behind her. "The back seat."

Rylie nodded and motioned to him, indicating that she would go to the other side of the car, and he should take the closer side, surrounding him. The danger was that Rene Scott definitely had a service weapon, and if he was cornered—and considering that he was a loose cannon—he might use it. They had to do this right.

They advanced quietly to the back doors of the car, and she whispered, "On three. One, two… three!"

They pulled open the doors at the same time and aimed their guns inside the car. "Don't move, Scott!" she shouted, as she was suddenly hit with a wall of smoky scent.

The smell of pot was so strong, it almost knocked her out. Her eyes watered. She waved her hand to cut through the haze and caught sight of the uniformed man sitting in the center of the back seat, his shirt opened to reveal his wiry chest hair. A scantily clad woman straddled his lap. They were both so stoned, they didn't even seem to notice the intrusion.

"Rene Scott," Michael barked. "What the hell?"

Rene glanced over at Michael, and then at Rylie, and started to giggle. "Look at that, would you, Ezzie? We got company!"

She started to giggle, too, throwing herself on Rene's chest.

Rylie leaned in and looked closer. The woman was certainly attractive, but she was probably about forty, and looked nothing like the photograph of Iona her best friend had showed them. Rene's service pistol was sitting on the seat next to him.

Rylie pulled out her badge. "Rylie Wolf, FBI. You're not where you're supposed to be, are you, Scott?"

He shook his head and burst into more laughter. The man certainly didn't look like an officer who took pride in his appearance. He was balding, with dark whiskers on his chin, and his uniform shirt had some unidentifiable orange-red stain on the collar, possibly the woman's lipstick. "I guess I'm not!"

"You turned off your scanner and radio, huh?" Michael said, shaking his head as the girl started to disentangle herself from the officer.

When she climbed out, she practically fell into Michael's arms. He steadied her. "And who might you be, tall, dark, and handsome?" she cooed, touching his collar flirtatiously.

"Why don't you let us ask the questions?" he said to her, making sure she was steady before letting go. "And you are?"

"Esther Havana, sweetie." She smiled, adjusting her short dress over her thighs. "Rene and I go *waaaaaay* back, don't we, darling?"

She leaned in and squeezed his cheek. He gazed up at her adoringly, then said, "Esther needed a ride. She was at a place in Clinton and had no way to get home. So I picked her up. I was just taking a break. You know, we all need breaks. Fifteen minutes."

"Fifteen minutes? I don't think so. Your radio has been off for at least an hour," Rylie pointed out, shaking her head. "And I get the feeling the chief of police won't be happy to hear what you've been up to."

He seemed to sober up almost immediately, because his eyes widened. "You're not going to tell him?"

She nodded and motioned to Michael, who pulled out his handcuffs. "We sure are. What did you do with Iona?"

"Who?"

So he was going to play dumb? Of course he was. "The girl. The hitchhiker you picked up. Curly blonde hair. Pretty, early twenties?"

He shook his head. "I don't know what the hell you're talking about. I been working, not picking up damn hitchhikers."

She stared at him, wondering whether to believe him. She didn't. "You're coming with us right now."

Rene started to complain, but she ignored it, setting her sights on the woman. She was likely a prostitute, but they had bigger fish to fry right now. “Sorry, Esther. We need to break up this party. You have a phone, you can call someone to pick you up?”

She already had a tube of lipstick out and was fixing her smile. “Oh, sure. My telling him I didn’t have a ride was just my excuse to spend some time with him, you know?”

He scowled at her as Michael yanked him out of the car and nudged him toward their vehicle.

Rylie stayed there, looking in the police car for any sign of Iona. Any sign that he might’ve had another girl with him prior to this. She went to the front seat and popped the trunk. She wandered into the field, away from the car. But there was nothing to see. No signs of the missing girl at all. If he’d caught her, he’d already gotten rid of the evidence.

Rene Scott had to be the killer, though. He had the right car. He was in the right location. He had a history of erratic behavior. If there was another guy out there who filled all those blanks so nicely, it’d be a hell of a coincidence. He’d also had the time, from when Lacey saw the car to now, to have gotten rid of the body before picking up Esther.

But as she followed Michael back to the truck, she really hoped they weren’t barking up the wrong tree again.

CHAPTER TWENTY FIVE

Rylie leaned against the table in the interrogation room and sucked down a sip of bitter coffee as she and Michael interrogated their latest suspect.

"This is bullshit," Rene Scott said, his cuffed hands piled on his lap like he was some kind of angel. "I didn't see or pick up any hitchhikers. You got the wrong person."

She opened the human resources file folder on Rene Scott and frowned. It was thick, and not just because he'd been on the force for thirty years. He had countless problems—complaints of mishandling suspects, losing evidence, sexism, racism, you name it. Every one of the charges had given him nothing more than a slap on the wrist. And why? Because he'd been carried along by a father who'd been chief of police. It gave her Bill Matthews vibes, so she couldn't help curling her lip in disgust.

"But you knew about the missing hitchhikers, didn't you?"

"Yeah. Sure. We all did. We also knew that they were bringing the FBI in to handle it, and we were to keep our hands off it." He lifted both hands from his lap and ran them through his thinning hair. "So I did. I did exactly like I was supposed to. I even saw a girl hitchhiking the day before and told her to get off the road, which is what we've been trained to do."

Rylie rolled her eyes. What a saint. It was almost shocking how much he sounded like Bill Matthews, blowing every tiny action he made into a heroic act while asking people to ignore his many glaring sins. "We're going to need to account for your movements, especially over the past few days."

"Yeah. That's easy. At least, for while I'm working. Headquarters logs where my car is at all times. That's probably how you found me, isn't it?"

She glanced at Michael. That was true. He might've been able to turn his radio off, but he couldn't disguise his location. "And you drive that car all the time?"

"Most of the time. Except when it goes to the shop."

"When you were driving your route, did you see a girl hitchhiking earlier today?"

He shook his head just as the door opened and Officer Bellamy poked his head in.

"But you were in that area, were you not? You saw the Volkswagen on the side of the road, broken down, didn't you?"

He nodded. "Called it in, too. Thought it was abandoned."

Bellamy leaned over and whispered something to Michael, who nodded and looked over at Rylie. "That checks out. He did make the call, shortly before he went radio silent."

She pressed her lips together. "And you didn't see anyone hitchhiking around there at all?"

He fixed her with a look that said that despite all these aspersions being cast upon his character, he was still a bit amused by it. It was the kind of look that said, *I know something you don't.*

Maybe he did know something. Or *someone*. A good lawyer who would sue the pants off her and make Kit Brandon hate her just as much as Bill Matthews had.

"I already told you. No." His voice was firm, final.

He's lying. At least, despite not wavering, every word that came out of his mouth felt false. There was something about his demeanor that seemed oily. But that was the way men like him always were. They seemed oily and untrustworthy even when they were telling the absolute truth.

Maybe he did make the call, but wasn't it suspicious that he turned off his radio right after reporting the abandoned car? Maybe he saw the car, saw the girl, turned off his radio, kidnapped her, took her someplace along his normal route, and killed her, all before picking up the prostitute? That would've been a busy few hours, but it could be done. "How can you prove it?"

Bellamy cleared his throat and held up a piece of paper. "We have his entire route in that car for the past few days. While he might have gone past the abandoned car today, he wasn't anywhere near where the other victims were found."

She wasn't about to let it go that easily. "Does he use that car every time? Maybe he switched out, used other vehicles… which accounts for the tire tracks being different every time."

Scott shook his head. "I was off during that last murder. I was home. All the way up in Scadduck. Heard about it when I was suiting up to come in."

"You live with someone who can vouch for you?" Rylie asked.

He shook his head and lifted his cuffed arms. "This is bullshit."

Bellamy looked him over and said, mostly to Michael, "Can I talk with you outside?"

Michael followed him out, and though she wasn't invited, Rylie followed, too. She hated being left out of these things. When Bellamy saw her, he frowned and leaned in to Michael's ear. Was he purposely trying to exclude her?

It didn't matter. Though she couldn't hear what Bellamy said, Michael shook his head and spoke for her to hear. "He's still our prime suspect."

Oh, so that was it. Despite the fact that Scott was a total scumbag, some of the guys on the force were rallying around him. She'd already gotten wind of that when they walked him into the precinct in handcuffs. The shock on their faces had quickly given way to outrage.

"You can't do that!" one of the officers there had shouted at them.

Scott had just smiled and shrugged in a charming way. "They're the feds. They think they can do anything they want. You know that."

Bellamy said, "Listen. He might have been caught in a bad space. But he's a good guy. Not some killer. I go hunting with him up at his lodge every winter. If you keep him any longer, it's going to put egg on your faces."

Rylie snorted. "Seriously? We caught him red-handed, on company time, smoking pot and screwing a prostitute. He deserves to get a little scrutiny, even just for that, don't you think?"

Bellamy's jaw tightened. He looked up and down the hallway. "You don't get it. He's not the type of guy you want to mess with. He's kind of untouchable."

Just like Bill Matthews. If there was one thing she hated, it was being told someone was untouchable. It made her want to poke that person all the more. Her fists clenched at her sides and she spat out, "Listen here, you—"

"Whoa, whoa, whoa," Michael said, stepping between them. "Thanks, Bell. We'll take all that under advisement."

Still glaring at her, Bellamy nodded, turned, and walked away.

She scowled at her partner. "Really? You really think it's okay that they all protect him like that, when he's a completely useless piece of—"

He fastened both hands on her shoulders. "Wolf. Calm down."

Rylie tried to yank herself lose. "Don't you tell me to—"

"Yeah, I'll tell you to calm down. Because you're about to get yourself into trouble for no reason. That guy in there?" He pointed to the interrogation room. "As much a scumbag as we both know he is, he's not our problem. I don't think he's our guy."

That was the last thing she wanted to hear. "But the car—"

"The fact is that unless he's going around switching cars in the middle of these abductions, it's highly unlikely. He wasn't even on duty during two of them. So you can waste your breath and energy wishing doom upon this person you already know is a waste of space, or we can go and find out who really killed those hitchhikers."

She sighed, her breathing returning to normal. Yes, as much as she didn't want to give up on Rene Scott, Michael did have a point. "But it's possible that he—"

"Yeah. It is. I'm not saying we let him go right now. But I think we need to build our case a bit more, because right now, it's about as sturdy as a house of cards." He thrust his hands into the pockets of his slacks and shrugged.

She looked around the precinct. Sure enough, some of the officers—even the ones that Brisbane had called his friends—were looking at them in disgust. "And how do you suggest we do that?"

"Like we always do. We keep digging. Meanwhile, we'll keep an eye on Scott. That's the best we can do."

"I just don't want anyone else to get hurt," she said softly.

He nodded. "Me neither. But—" He stopped talking abruptly as something over her head caught his attention.

She spun to find Hoskins motioning to him, a grim look on his face. Michael strode down the hallway toward him, and Rylie followed. "What is it?"

"It's that girl, the blonde whose car broke down," he said in a low voice. "I just got a call. They found her body about ten minutes ago."

"And?" Michael asked, as they all seemed to hold their breath.

"Same as before. Hit on the head, strangled. This one was dumped on the side of the road near that rest stop."

"Grand Fork?" Michael asked.

Hoskins nodded grimly, his mouth a straight line. "Yep. Weren't you just around there?"

Near the rest stop. And yes, Hoskins was right. It was almost *exactly* where they'd been, only an hour ago. They'd been so close.

Not only that, if it was close to the rest stop, which also wasn't very far from the abandoned car, it meant that Rene Scott could have had plenty of time to kill the girl, dump the body, and pick up Esther Havana.

The despair she felt at that news gave way almost immediately to white-hot anger. She exchanged a glance with Michael and then said to Hoskins, “Keep Scott in custody for now. Come on, Bris, let’s get out there.”

CHAPTER TWENTY SIX

By the time Rylie pulled to the shoulder of the road where the police car was already parked, lights flashing, it was dark.

Grim-faced, she pulled off her seatbelt and looked around. The sign for the Grand Fork rest stop was visible in her rearview mirror. It was that close. Meaning it was entirely possible that with some crafty planning, Rene Scott could've committed this crime.

But if he hadn't…

"He's speeding up," Michael said, staring out the window at the police officers gathered around the latest victim. "Snatching a victim almost every few hours. He didn't even wait for nighttime for this one."

She nodded and stepped out of the car, knowing exactly what that meant. It meant that, if Rene Scott wasn't their man, no hitchhiker would be safe tonight.

They had to nail down this killer, and soon.

"If he's speeding up, he's going to make mistakes," she said to him as they walked along the shoulder of the road. "I just hope we're around to catch him in one of them."

"Yeah," Brisbane said. The group of officers parted to let them through.

The girl was lying face up, almost as if sunbathing, blood in a halo around her wild, curly hair. One of her ballet flats was missing. Her face was peaceful and unblemished. She looked as if she might just be sleeping. Rylie gritted her teeth. It was definitely the girl from the photo. Iona.

She turned to the police officer who'd found the body, a young kid who looked like he hadn't yet gotten out of high school. His Adam's apple bobbed in his stick-thin neck as he said, "Looks like she got out of the car around here."

He pointed, the police car's headlights illuminating the scene before them. Sure enough, there were tire marks there, and petite footprints. Then… a single shoe, lying abandoned in the dirt. She crouched in front of it. "Looks like signs of a struggle."

Just like before. She'd gotten in the car with him, then for whatever reason, he'd pulled over and let them out along a deserted stretch of road. Then he'd hit them, rendering them too weak to fight as he choked the life out of them.

But if this was anything like the other case, there'd be no DNA left behind. No clues to go on. The killer likely wore gloves, covered his tracks. Knew exactly how to avoid detection. That's another reason why Rene Scott was their suspect. He knew how to stay out of their way.

But then why had he called attention to himself by screwing a prostitute near the murder sight? That had taken a lot of guts.

The questions in this case just continued to pile up, making her feel dizzy. Rylie swallowed and blinked, trying to get her head back into the game. "The medical examiner on his way?"

The officer nodded.

"You find any other clues? See any other vehicles in the area?"

He shook his head.

Rylie sighed and ran a hand down her face. The more she did this, the more she felt like she was riding on a broken record, going through the same things over and over again, with no different result. She looked at Michael, hoping he had something new to add.

But he looked just as grim and confused as she felt. He said, "I guess Scott could've done this."

"That's what I was thinking. But…"

"If he did, why was he at the rest stop? Why didn't he try to get as far away from the body as possible?"

"Bingo," she mumbled, glad he was so in tune with her. She didn't feel like having to explain it. She was starting to get a headache.

"I don't know. Maybe he was high. Maybe he was horny and wanted to stop for a little play. There's still a possibility he's our guy. But if he's not…"

She walked away before he could say more, because she didn't want to hear it. She knew it, deep down, and the thought made her stomach turn. *If he's not, he could be searching for his next victim right now.*

She looked up and down the road. It was after nine in the evening, still early enough that there were a few cars passing by now and then. Still early enough that he might find his hitchhiker somewhere on this road. They had to make sure that didn't happen. Somehow.

"Bris," she said, whirling back to him. "Call Hoskins. Tell him to put all his manpower on the road right now. If there's anyone alone and walking the highway, I want them picked up and brought to headquarters. They shouldn't be out here."

He nodded. "All right. Makes sense. And?"

As soon as the words left her lips, something occurred to her. If the police stepped up their efforts and they took all the hitchhikers off the road, the killer might be scared off. He might run somewhere else, and they'd never be able to catch him.

Michael had already brought his phone to his ear, but she grabbed it and ended the call. "On second thought, let's think about this."

"Think about what, Wolf? We want this guy to stop."

She shook her head. "No, that's not all we want. Because you know he *won't* stop. He's not sane. If we pull all of the hitchhikers off the road, he might stop out of necessity. But he'll just move somewhere else. We don't just want him to stop. We want him *caught*."

"Okay. And…" he said, uncertainly, his eyes narrowing. "How do we—"

"I think I might have an idea."

He shook his head slowly. "Why am I thinking I am not going to like it?"

"You don't have to like it. You just have to help me with it. As my partner."

"If it's anything dangerous…"

"Bris. That's the nature of our job. You didn't sign up to pet puppies. You signed up to be an agent of the FBI. Right?"

"Right, but…" He started to shake his head, but then he noticed something down the road once again, over her head. He squinted. "Wait…What the hell is that?"

She whirled and saw a form, walking slowly down the shoulder of the road in the darkness. It wasn't a member of the police force, that was for sure. From what she could see, it was a female, with long, dark hair to her waist.

"A hitchhiker," Michael said. "And you're right. We need to get them off the—"

"Wait." She strained to see in the dark. There was something wrong about the girl. She wasn't simply walking. She was limping, head down, treading what wasn't a straight line, the empty landscape behind her. A couple of times, she nearly staggered into the road. "Something's wrong with her."

Without hesitation, Rylie took off in a sprint. The closer she got, the more she saw. The girl's face was covered in dirt and blood. She seemed listless, as if walking in a dream, and she wasn't carrying a bag. Her shirt was torn and she had scrapes on her face. She didn't even notice Rylie until she was right on top of her. The girl practically tried to walk through her. Rylie had to reach out and hold her to stop her.

"Hey. What are you doing here?"

She looked up, startled, eyes wide and full of fear. Then she murmured something incomprehensible—was it in Spanish?—and tried to continue walking past her.

"Hey," Michael said, joining Rylie. The woman didn't look up, so he snapped his fingers. "Young lady. What happened to you?"

The girl blinked, and some clarity seemed to come back to her, because she said, in heavily accented English, "He tried to take me. I fight him. And I get away."

"Who?" Rylie asked.

She trembled. "A man. He say he was a policeman, but he was not. I know that. He thinks he's one, but he do bad things. Very bad things."

A policeman.

And yet another crime. Murdering a girl whose car had broken down. Messing around with a prostitute. And now… what? Assaulting another hitchhiker?

Seemed like Rene Scott had had a very busy afternoon.

"It's all right, miss," Michael said, pulling out his credentials. "We're from the FBI."

The girl glanced at it and flinched. Rylie understood. The policeman had probably done the same thing, promised to help her, to be someone she could trust. And she'd just gone through what was possibly the most terrifying experience of her life.

Rylie took over, flashing her own credentials. "He's telling the truth. You're safe. But we need to find the man who did this to you. Let's go somewhere, get you cleaned up, and you can tell us everything."

CHAPTER TWENTY SEVEN

Rylie stood near the back of the open doors of the ambulance, watching an EMT treat the scrapes on the hitchhiker's forehead. She pulled the blanket tighter around her body as she sucked down lukewarm coffee from the EMT's thermos. She stared straight ahead, her lower lip trembling.

They'd asked her a few questions before treatment—her name was Marta Flores, and she'd said she was an exchange student from Spain. Apparently, there'd been some problems with her host family, and she'd decided to run off. Not exactly a glowing first experience in America, that was for sure.

When the EMT was done, he took Michael and Rylie a few steps away and said, "It appears she's in mild shock. She should be all right with some rest."

Michael nodded as he looked at the girl. "I spoke to Hos. We obviously don't want to send her back to the host family. The police will put her up in a hotel while we see if we can get in touch with the exchange student program."

As the EMT stepped away, Rylie said, "Whatever she's been through, it's got to be related to the case. A policeman."

"Yeah. You're thinking Rene Scott?"

"Only one way to find out for sure." They started to approach the girl, but Rylie stopped. "You should probably let me take the lead on this. Because of what she's been through…"

"Yeah." He held back. "By all means. If we can get the name for the exchange student program, I'll start making calls."

Rylie nodded and stepped over to the girl. "Hi, Marta? I'm Rylie Wolf. I know it's been a difficult night for you, but I was wondering if you'd answer some questions?"

She nodded warily.

"Great. We want to get you someplace safe. Can you give us the name of the exchange student program you used?"

She shook her head. "I am not going back with that family."

"Oh, no. We don't expect you to. But if we can get in touch with the program, they'll be able to get in touch with your family and make alternate arrangements for you. We need you to be safe, obviously. I'm sure they'll take care of you. Did you lose all your luggage? Your passport?"

She nodded.

"All right. We'll try to get them back. Do you remember the name of the exchange student place you went through?"

She shook her head.

"Hmm," Rylie said, pulling out her phone. She typed something in with her thumb. "Maybe if I name them, you'll remember? Let's see. We have ESG, Exchange Students International, International Students Group…"

She tucked a lock of dark hair behind her ear. "International Students Group," she said softly. "That one."

Rylie looked back at Michael, who gave her a thumbs-up as he brought the phone to his ear. "Okay, great. I'm so sorry this happened to you. Do you think you can speak a little about exactly what happened?"

"*Sí*. I was walking along the road and a man in a police car come. He tell me I can no walk on side of road. So I tell him I must. He say he take me in. Then he tell me he take me to next town. He not a nice man. Very strange."

"Strange how?"

"Just always looking in the back mirror. And I see his badge. It's not real. Looks like something—like something a boy get in a toy chest. Cheap. Like play games?" She pointed to her pocket. "Yours real. His, *not* real."

Rylie blinked, trying to understand. If it had been Rene Scott, the man had an actual police badge. "Can you tell me what he looked like?"

"Short hair like yours in color. Brown." She touched the low ponytail resting on Rylie's shoulder. "Good face. Handsome. Not fat. Not thin. Just right. Very tall. I think I like him, first time I see him. But when I get in the car, I no like him."

Rylie looked back to see if Michael had heard any of that. But he was still pacing in the lights of one of the police cars, the phone up to his ear. *Nothing* about that description sounded like Rene Scott at all. Scott was balding, with salt-and-pepper hair, a beer belly, and his bulbous nose and protruding jaw weren't what many would call handsome.

This wasn't good.

If what Marta was saying was correct, it meant that the killer was still out there.

"So you got into the car with him—a police car?"

She nodded.

"Unmarked?" When the girl looked at her in confusion, she said, "Did it have any writing on the sides? The doors? Lights? Like those?"

Marta followed her pointed finger to one of the squad cars. She shook her head. "Nothing on doors. But *sí*, it had lights. And color different. Black."

"Black?"

She nodded.

Rylie's mouth opened. So, an entirely different car than they'd been looking for. "What happened then?"

"I ask him to pull over. He say no. I fight with him. Car go…" She mimed a car going off the road. "Crash! Big crash!"

Rylie's eyes widened. "Where is this? Close by?"

She motioned down the road. "That way. Might be. I don't know. I climb out of car and run while he no looking. I hide in trees, he don't see me, then walk for long time. I don't know. I hear tires. I think he drive away."

Rylie straightened. So a black car with obvious damage, it sounded like. This was something they could go on. *Unless*, of course, he was constantly changing vehicles, which also sounded like a possibility.

"All right," Rylie said, looking at her notes. "This is helpful. I—"

"Wolf."

She looked back to find Michael motioning her over, a concerned expression on his face. She held up a finger to Marta. "One moment, please."

She hurried down the embankment toward him, still looking over her notes. "This is very interesting. I don't think it's Scott. I think it might be—" She stopped when she realized how confused he looked. "What's wrong?"

"Well, it's the damnedest thing. I just got off the phone with that International Students Group."

"And?"

"They don't have a record of anyone named Marta Flores. And they haven't sent anyone from Spain to Montana in their program for *years*."

"Okay, so maybe she just forgot the name of the—"

"I think we need to put in a call to ICE."

She froze, her line of thinking completely disrupted. Of course, it made sense. "Okay, maybe. If she's in the country illegally, then we can hand her over to them and wash our hands of her. But she's been our most helpful witness so far. She gave me a description of the guy, and—"

"And she could be a criminal. Who knows, she might be working with him. Did you see her gun?"

Rylie's jaw dropped. "What gun?" She glanced back at the girl, who was watching them intently.

"She had it strapped to her calf. I saw it just a second ago. Her pants leg rode up as she was sitting on the tailgate of the ambulance," he whispered. "I don't think International Students Group allows weapons."

She gritted her teeth. She hated missing things. How had she missed that? Usually, she was so skeptical of everyone, and that was what made her a good agent. Maybe it was because now, every time she saw an injured girl, a young woman who needed her help, she thought of Maren. She let her own past get in the way. And she needed to stop that, to harden herself against it. *Everyone,* even young girls, had the potential to be criminals.

"All right, all right. But that's not our problem. I have a few more questions to ask her. She's been really helpful, so if you could just—"

"Shit!" Michael shouted, suddenly breaking into a run, past her.

She whirled to find the back of the ambulance empty. Marta was gone.

She took off after Michael, but with his long strides, he easily outpaced her, running far ahead into the darkness. But suddenly, he stopped, and she nearly ran straight into his shoulder blades. "What? Where is she?"

Out of breath, he scanned the darkness. "I don't know. I don't see her anywhere."

Rylie spun in a circle, searching the woods around them. Marta was gone.

She pounded her fist against her thigh. "Dammit!" She waved it away. "Well, she's the least of our concerns right now. We have bigger fish to fry."

Michael dragged his hands down his face. "You think what she was telling you was the truth, though?"

Rylie nodded. "I do. She said the guy had a fake badge. He was tall with brown hair, nothing like Rene Scott. And that he'd been driving a black car, unmarked, but with police lights on top."

"That's interesting. So, Rene isn't our guy, then?"

"I don't think so. And that means he's still out there. So we've got to move fast."

He nodded and started to jog toward the side of the road. "Right. I'll call Hoskins and tell him to put the whole highway force on high alert, and that we need to scrub the area of all hitchhikers."

"No. Wait. That's not what I mean."

He stopped, wincing. She could already tell he was wary. "What *do* you mean, then?"

"I told you I had a plan."

"And that's what scares me." He motioned her forward with both hands. "All right. Give it to me."

"Come here." She climbed the embankment toward the road, then went to the police car and grabbed one of the paper maps of the area from the front passenger seat. She laid it out on the hood of the car, grabbed her pen from behind her ear, and pointed. "Look. This is where Gary Blake was dumped. This exit is where Candy Fronheiser was dumped. And here is where Iona was dumped. Around here is likely where Marta was picked up." She circled the whole area. "It's a relatively small area."

"One that we can easily contain," Michael said with a nod.

"By *contain*, you mean stopping him from striking again. But we want him to strike again, so we can catch him."

He stared at her in the dim light from the police car's headlights. When realization dawned, he shook his head. "Don't tell me…"

"Yes," she said with a nod. "We'll *make* him strike again. By using me as bait."

CHAPTER TWENTY EIGHT

Rylie stared at her partner, waiting for his answer. She didn't need it; she was planning to go through with it anyway. But his support would've been nice.

"No," he said simply, finally, like a stern father who'd been pushed too hard by his teenage daughter.

She smiled. "Too bad your vote doesn't count."

"Oh, it doesn't? Then why did you bother telling me?"

"Because while you may think that it's crazy—and you may be right about it—if you think about it a little more, you'll realize that it's the best way to catch him. Maybe the only way."

He shook his head. "You don't need to make yourself bait. What are you trying to prove? You're proving nothing to nobody if you're dead—just that you're a dumbass. We could—"

"Wait for him to strike again? News flash—we have been doing that. And a bang-up job it's been so far. Right now, he's leaving a trail of bodies."

"And the trail of bodies will lead us right to him, if we—"

"I don't want any more of them. If we put me out there, it ends. Tonight." She stared at him, holding his gaze. He attempted to look away, but she put a hand on his forearm. "You can't tell me you don't want that."

He let out a sigh. "Yeah, of course I want that. I just wish there was some easier way. Some way where you're not in so much danger. It's a hell of a risk."

She smiled. "Well, you're not cute enough. He probably wouldn't pick you up."

He matched her smile, but barely. "All right. So how do we do this?"

Rylie looked down at herself. In her blazer, jeans, and severe ponytail, she looked exactly like what she was—a middle-aged woman. Michael didn't say as much, but he had to be thinking it—*she* wasn't exactly his normal victim, either.

She slipped out of the blazer, noticing one of the EMTs was wearing a flannel shirt jacket. "Hey!" she called to him. "Can I borrow that?"

The EMT nodded and jogged it over to her.

She slipped it on. Taking the band out of her hair, she scraped her hair into a higher ponytail. Then she turned around for his approval.

"You think this is a good enough fudge?" she asked him.

He frowned. "Those Easy Spirits kind of give you away."

"Hey. They're not Easy Spirits!" she said, looking down at her black lace-up boots that until that moment, she'd thought were stylish as well as comfortable. "They're popular with young people, too."

"Uh-huh," he said doubtfully.

She waved him away. "Doesn't matter. This isn't an Aeropostale fashion show. It's going to be dark. Do I look like someone he'd pick up or not?"

He inspected her and nodded. "I guess you do."

She rolled her eyes. "Thanks for the vote of confidence, Bris."

"I'm voting no confidence in this one," he mumbled, shaking his head. "I don't think it's a good idea."

"We're past the idea stage now, Bris. It's happening. So the least you can do is play along."

"All right. Where do you want me?"

She handed him her car keys. "Park somewhere at the next exit."

"Next exit?" He stared at her like she'd just announced she was going to hitchhike to the moon. "That's like, ten miles down the road. If something happens, I won't know. I won't even be able to get to you—"

"Calm down. It's okay. What do we know about this guy, based on the previous murders?"

He shrugged. "What do you mean? He's a lunatic. We can't trust him. He'll hit you over the head when you're least expecting it and—"

"No, what we know is that he never kills right away. He takes his victims in his car first. I get the feeling he likes to play good cop. He likes having the authority over these people. So he takes his time, making them sweat first, thinking they're in trouble. That's what Marta said. He picked her up and told her she wasn't supposed to be hitchhiking. Then he said he'd drive her to the next exit. So he pretends to be their savior, and then he kills them. It's a game to him."

Michael swallowed. "And you want to put yourself in his way."

"Yes. It should be perfectly safe. I have my phone. I'll text you if he picks me up."

"But what if I can't get to you in time? What if I can't—"

"You will. Just alert Hoskins that this is the plan, all right? So that the other officers stay out of our way but know to come in if we need them."

He sighed. "Yeah. If you say so."

The ambulance pulled off down the road, and the police officers got into their cars to follow. Soon, this area of the deserted highway would be quiet and still once again.

And it would be time for her to try to catch a killer.

*

Rylie walked alone in the darkness, putting one foot in front of the other.

Okay, maybe Michael was right. Maybe these shoes aren't as fashionable as I thought.

But other things Michael had said also played in a never-ending loop in her mind. *It's too dangerous. What if I can't get to you in time? What are you trying to prove?*

She knew exactly what she was trying to prove. How many times in the past twenty years had she wished she could've been braver, to go out of her hiding place and confront those murderers who'd taken Maren? Or, at the very least, she wished it was her out there, instead of Maren. If so, things would've been different. So now, here she was, trading places with the next victim, opening herself up to the same sort of terror she knew her sister had gone through.

In a way, deep down, she knew she was punishing herself. It was probably why she'd always acted so recklessly, why Bill Matthews had been driven up a wall by her. Action, any action, even dangerous action, was what she had to do to make up for her inaction twenty years ago.

She sighed as she looked up and down the highway. It was almost daunting, how desolate and empty the landscape was. From here, it felt like she was the only person left in the world, among the rising rock formations and scraggly pine trees. The highway cut a winding path across the landscape, the only man-made thing in view. A few cars had passed since she'd last seen Michael. He'd hopped into the truck, beeping the horn at her before heading off at his normal, turtle-like speed. She couldn't see him, but she knew he'd been watching her in the rearview mirror until she disappeared from view.

Every time a car passed, she stuck out her thumb, but so far, no takers.

She heard the sound of tires on asphalt coming closer before she saw the headlights, illuminating the darkness around her. She turned, and sure enough, a car was coming closer. From the headlights, it looked like a sedan.

She quickly put her thumb out, holding it there as she walked backward.

The car whizzed by, just like the three that had come before it.

She lowered her arm and continued moving, wondering if this would be worth it at all. It was already after midnight, and getting colder by the second. Her breath was starting to puff out in front of her, in a warm white cloud.

She pulled the flannel shirt tighter around her frame. Maybe the killer had gotten into that accident with Marta, sped off, and decided to call it a day. He'd gotten bolder, attacking two girls in one day. He'd probably been feeling invincible, and the incident with Marta had probably thrown a pretty big wrench in his plans. Maybe he'd decided to hang up his gloves permanently. Maybe this was a waste of time.

No. His brain was infected. He'd never be able to stay away. Maybe for a day or two. But he'd be back.

When he came back, she'd be here. She'd take this route tomorrow. And the next day. She'd walk this highway as long as she had to, until he picked her up.

Her phone suddenly lit up with a text. It was from Michael. *Ok?*

She stopped walking to type in: *Yes. No luck so far.*

All right. Keep me posted.

At least he hadn't tried to throw a roadblock in her way, like Bill Matthews. She had to appreciate that. As dangerous as Michael knew it was, he'd known when to step back. To let her do what she was going to do.

Her thoughts turned to Cooper Rich. *I asked for this assignment. Because I wanted to see you. I missed you, Rylie.*

And what had she done? Stared at him stupidly and then just awkwardly walked away. She should've said something else to him, something nice, but it was so unexpected. He'd never said anything so sweet to her in Seattle. Had absence really made his heart grow fonder? Possibly.

The truth was, she had trust issues.

She wanted to trust him, and he'd never given her a reason to doubt him before. But she'd never been good with relationships, and opening up, especially with men. That was why Joe had left her. He'd called her a "closed book." And that, she decided, was fine, because she wasn't interested in opening herself up. That only brought pain.

No… the reason she and Cooper had never gotten together was because they'd always moved in totally different circles. Even then, in Seattle. And especially now that she was in the Midwest.

She had a different life now. There was no point in wasting time thinking about something that couldn't happen.

Rylie was so deep in her thoughts that she almost didn't notice the approaching headlights until they were practically on top of her.

In the last possible moment, she stuck out her thumb.

The car, a burgundy sedan, passed by her, and then the brake lights went red. It navigated to the side of the road.

It had worked.

Smoothing the top of her ponytail, she ran to catch up with the waiting car.

It was only when she reached the back bumper that she noticed the giant antenna protruding from the top of the trunk. She'd seen things like that on unmarked police cars. It belonged to a scanner.

Taking a deep breath, she went to the passenger's side window as it powered down. She looked inside to find a man smiling at her.

Neat, brownish hair. Big, dark eyes. Handsome. And was that a uniform he was wearing?

This was it. Exactly what she'd been fishing for.

Her heart pounded in her chest. Was this man—this fairly normal-looking, everyday man—a sadistic killer? Had those hands, currently wrapped around the steering wheel, used an instrument to bludgeon a poor victim into senselessness?

With that thought, her skin popped with goosebumps, and once again, she thought of Michael's words: *It's too dangerous.*

"Hi!" she said, somehow remembering to act youthfully.

"Hey, there. Did I see you looking for a ride, pretty girl?"

She nodded.

"Where you headed?"

"Oh, just as far as you are willing to take me," she said, forcing a girlish giggle. "I'm just trying to get away. To Idaho?"

"Yep. Sounds like I'm your man. Hop in." The sound of the door locks clicked.

"Back or front?" she asked.

"Either way."

She opened the back door and climbed in behind him. As she settled in, he said, "What's your name, honey?"

"I'm Brandy," she said, probably because she was thinking of alcohol. At that moment, she could've used a stiff drink.

"Jeff. Where you from?" he said, glancing in the rearview mirror. Their eyes locked there, and she wondered if he was scrutinizing her face to see how old she was.

She gnawed on her lip to give the illusion of someone more youthful. "I'm from Story."

"Story… I know that place. You're from there? Small town."

She nodded and blew into her hands, not because they were cold but because it covered her face a bit. He was still scrutinizing her. She made her voice extra high and girlish, as she said, "Nice to meet you. Thanks. It was getting really cold out there."

She expected he'd shift the car into drive and head off, but he stayed there, smiling at her. "I'll bet. But I'm sorry. You're not going to like what I have to say."

"Oh?" she asked, wondering where this was going. She hoped she wasn't wrong with what she'd told Michael, about him waiting to kill his next victim. She discreetly felt for her gun at her side, hoping she wouldn't have to use it yet. "I'm not?"

"Unfortunately not." Then he turned and showed it to her, slowly enough that she could see what it was, but not slowly enough that she could take in its quality. A golden badge.

"What's that?" she asked, feigning confusion as she pulled her hand from the gun underneath her flannel. "Are you a…?"

"A cop?" He nodded, a proud smile on his face. "Sure am. And I hate to tell you, but hitchhiking's not only really dangerous, it's also illegal in these parts. I'm going to have to take you in."

Her mouth made the shape of an O, and she brought a hand to it. She wondered if this was how he'd lured all his other victims in. Marta had said something similar. So he'd changed out the car, somehow, and now he was here, trying to make up for his last disappointment, the victim that got away.

"What? Are you sure? You mean, I'm under arrest?" she asked, her voice higher-pitched and squeakier than she was used to.

He nodded.

"I'm going to jail?"

He nodded again.

She reached for the door handle. "Oh, no, please. I can just go…" She pulled on it, noting it was locked. He'd made sure of that. He wasn't going to let her go as easily as he'd lost Marta.

His tone of voice changed, becoming gruffer. Scarier. "I'm sorry, but you can't. You're under arrest. And if you just sit there nicely, I won't cuff you."

Quickly, she attempted to whip up some fake tears, but they wouldn't come, so she covered her face in her hands and pretended to sob. "Oh no, this is terrible! I have never been arrested before."

His voice softened just the slightest bit. "Well, I can't just let you go, honey. You have to be taught a lesson. And it's my job to do just that. I wouldn't be worth anything if I didn't do my job, right?"

She calculated her next words very carefully. He got off on being in charge. On using his authority. So she knew just what he'd like to hear. Begging.

"But Jeff, please… sir. I won't do it again. I promise."

There was a long pause, where he seemed to consider this, but she got the feeling from the smile on his face that he'd been through this script many times before. That he was actually *enjoying* seeing her twist in the wind, completely and totally at his mercy. "You do? Are you sure?"

She nodded, her face buried in her hands. Somewhere in her mind, it occurred to her to text Michael. To tell him that she'd found the killer. But she couldn't do it now. She thought about pulling out her gun, arresting him on the spot, but she wanted to see what he would do. And yes, maybe a little sick part of her wanted to play with him, just like he was playing with her.

He sighed, and the next time he spoke, his voice was gentle and calm. "Hey, okay. What about this? As long as you promise me you'll never do it again, I'll let you off with a warning."

"Really?" She clasped her hands together. "Oh, thank you!"

He wagged his finger at her. "But you have to promise me you'll never do it again."

"I promise." She crossed her heart and held her hand up in an oath.

"All right. But you can't stay here on the highway. I need to take you to the next exit. You can find a place to stay, then call someone and have them pick you up. You understand?"

She nodded. “Thank you. Just so much, thank you,” she gushed.

He turned back to the front of the car and shifted to drive, then pulled out onto the highway.

Grabbing her phone, she quietly texted Michael: *Bingo. In the car now.*

CHAPTER TWENTY NINE

Michael Brisbane sat in the parking lot of an abandoned gas station at the highway exit, staring at the GPS scanner.

Rylie hadn't texted. And yet, her GPS showed her stopped, and then, suddenly, moving at a high rate of speed toward him.

A second later, the text came in: *Bingo. In the car now.*

Shit. He'd really hoped that the killer would've decided to take the rest of the night off. Apparently not.

He quickly thumbed in: *Watching you. I'll be ready.*

Though he didn't expect her to respond, he spent the next thirty seconds watching the screen.

Then he pulled out of the gravel lot and headed toward the on-ramp, so he could be ready. As he did, a strange foreboding filled him, a feeling something wasn't right. And it wasn't. This idea was damn stupid. Suicidal, even.

But that was Rylie. He'd only known her two months, but he knew that. She always went balls to the wall, throwing herself into every case as if she had something to prove. Playing dangerous. One day, it was going to catch up with her.

He only hoped it wasn't today. On his watch.

As he parked on the overpass, with a perfect view so he could see when the car approached, he cursed himself. He should be doing more. What was he doing, sitting here, playing back-up? That wasn't his style.

But it wasn't Rylie's either. One of them had to sit in the back seat. And because of her trauma, because she always felt like she needed to prove herself after everything that happened to her, he felt the need to step back and let her take the reins.

He wouldn't be able to do that for long. He'd joined the FBI because he had his own demons, and at the time, this had felt like the best way to exorcize them. He *needed* to exorcize them, and sitting in the shadows, letting other people take control, wasn't going to do it.

He followed the blinking red dot on the GPS tracker, watching it draw closer and closer to the clover leaf that made up the ramp to the exit where he waited. Any minute now, he expected the lights of the car's headlights to appear in view. If it stopped, he was ready to jump on the gas and race there.

But it didn't stop. No, it was much worse than that.

It simply *disappeared.* One second, it was blinking, and then, suddenly, it just blinked off, leaving nothing but a sea of black.

He stared at it, rubbing his eyes. He grabbed the screen and stared at it, thinking it was just in a bad location. But the more he stared without seeing it reappear, the tighter he clenched his jaw.

Dammit. He'd known something like this would happen. No wonder he'd been having that bad feeling. Why was it that, no matter how many times he felt that way, he always ignored the feeling, even though it had never failed him? He needed to listen to his intuition more often.

Desperate, he jumped out of the car and ran to the railing on the overpass, searching the highway for those headlights, willing them to appear.

But they didn't.

Other than a few trucks heading in the opposite direction, their red taillights silent and steady, the highway was completely dark.

"Shit," he said aloud, running for his vehicle. He jumped in and sent another text: *Where the hell are you? The GPS isn't working.*

Then he raced onto the highway, blasting his way through a stop sign, something he never did. As he passed it, he checked the GPS. No blinking light. No sign of her at all. It was as if she had simply vanished, but he knew it would probably be even worse than that.

He had to get to her last known location before something terrible happened.

*

Watching you. I'll be ready.

Rylie's phone was buried under layers of flannel, visible only to her. She knew she shouldn't keep looking at it, but she couldn't help it. Michael's message was the only thing that gave her comfort as she sat in the back of the car, listening to "Sweet Home Alabama" on the radio as Jeff barreled down the highway, reaching speeds of nearly one hundred miles per hour.

It was fine, as long as he didn't try to stop, she told herself, fingering the gun at her hip, under the bulky flannel. *Relax. Prepare for what you have to do.*

"You like this song?" he asked her, turning it up.

She nodded. "Sure. Everyone likes this song," she said, wondering if it gave away her age. It didn't matter anymore. He'd taken the bait.

But she still didn't want him to suspect anything was amiss.

So she giggled, high-pitched, in a way that would've annoyed her had she heard anyone else do it. "I don't know who sings it, though. I don't know all these old-time singers."

He chuckled. "Lynyrd Skynyrd."

"Oh right. You been a police officer long?"

"All my life. Probably longer than you've been alive."

That definitely wasn't true—he was only about ten years her senior—but it was good to know the ruse was working. She giggled some more, as the sign for the exit came into view. Ten miles away. Somewhere out there, Michael was waiting. "Are you dropping me off at the exit?"

He didn't speak right away. Then he said, "Yep. That all right?"

"Sure. I hope there's a place to eat there. I'm kind of hungry. And I don't really know who I'd call," she went on, babbling for the sake of stopping herself from trembling. "All my family's pretty far away in Story. They'll be pissed I ran out on them."

"You ran out on them?" He seemed amused.

"Yeah. I always wanted to hitchhike across the country. I just didn't know it was illegal," she said with another giggle. "Oh well, I made it one state, at least. I should give myself a pat on the back for that. Huh?"

"Sure," he said, his hands moving over the controls in the front seat. What was he doing? "Don't you worry, we'll be there any second now, and then you can give them a call."

Great. She knew that was a lie. He wasn't taking her anywhere safe. But where was Michael? He was keeping track of her on the GPS. She thought he'd be here by now.

"Thanks," she said, touching the butt of her gun.

She glanced at her phone to see another message from Michael: *Where the hell are you? The GPS isn't working.*

She looked up, and when she did, through the dim light in the car's cabin, she saw his face in the rearview mirror glaring at her. "Everything all right?" he asked.

No. No, it was not. She wasn't naïve to think that the non-working GPS was because of crappy satellite reception in this area. No, there was something on Jeff's face that told her everything. He'd done this, scrambled the signal somehow.

Which meant one terrifying thing: He was on to her.

The sign for the next exit appeared, now two miles away.

Without warning, he slammed on the gas, sending her head back against the headrest. Clearly, he had no intention of stopping there.

Forget Michael. She'd have to handle this herself.

CHAPTER THIRTY

"What are you doing?" Rylie said innocently as she watched the overpass come into view. "Why are we not stopping?"

"I think you know why," he said with a chuckle.

"No, I don't."

He smiled. "I don't think you're being absolutely straight with me."

She knew he'd call her out on that, but she still stiffened. "What do you mean? I've been straight with you." She giggled. "You were the one who wasn't straight with me, pretending to give me a ride and then telling me you were a police officer."

His smile fell. "Don't give me that. You think I didn't notice the gun in your shirt?"

Her fingers wrapped around the handle.

"You think I don't know who you are? You might think you're clever, playing the naïve young girl, but trust me, it's not working." He was flooring the gas pedal, now, reaching speeds of over 120 miles per hour. "And guess what? That gun isn't going to protect you."

She pulled it out and aimed it at him.

It had no effect at all. When she realized that, he laughed. "I don't know your name, but I'm betting you're law enforcement? Federal? FBI, maybe? I heard on the scanner that they were coming in."

"Pull over," she ground out.

He chuckled. "Sorry… Brandy, which I'm sure is not your real name, just as Jeff isn't mine. But the thing is, I'm perfectly content to crash this car and kill both of us. So shoot me if you want. We'll both die, and it won't bother me at all."

He was insane. Absolutely insane. And she knew that he had the power. She could order him around all she wanted, but if he had a death wish, he could easily kill them both. "Why are you doing this?"

He smiled as he stared straight ahead. "It's my duty."

"You're a police officer?"

"I tried to be one. They wouldn't let me, because of my issues. Because I'd spent some of my youth in mental institutions. Can you believe that? It's their damn fault. And I'm a better upholder of the law than any one of them." His lips curled into a snarl, and he spat out his next words. "Better than you. That's for damn sure."

"Why were you in mental institutions?"

"My sister, Eloise. She died. She was murdered. She picked up a damn hitchhiker right around here, just trying to be nice. And what did she get for it? Robbed, her throat slit, left to rot on the side of the road while the killer took off with her car. After that, my family fell apart. They ignored me. All because of one scumbag. He ruined my life." More spitting, pounding the steering wheel with his fist.

Rylie thought of Maren. After her disappearance and her mother's murder, the same had happened to her family. Things like that have a way of leaving an awful, irreparable hole in a family. "Did he go to jail?"

"No. They never caught him. Goddamn hitchhiker, a good-for-nothing homeless nomad, wandering from place to place."

Ah, now it was starting to make sense. "I see. So that's why you killed the others, then?"

He nodded. "Sure as hell. The police around these parts don't do nothing. Just let them go. And every time I went out on the highway, there were more and more of them. They don't follow the rules. They're dangerous. They need to be stopped. So it was up to me to stop them. For Eloise."

"Your sister."

The dark outlines of trees were passing by in a blur at breakneck speed. "Yeah. My sister. She was ten years my senior, and a good girl. She looked after me. She had her whole life ahead of her, and that man took her from us. Ruined everything. I couldn't take it. My parents finally put me in an institution, to save me from myself."

Rylie nodded, trying to be sympathetic. "I understand what that can do. I had a sister who disappeared, too. Decades ago. Not a day goes by that I don't wonder what happened to her."

He lifted an eyebrow. "You never wanted to do something to get back at whoever took her?"

She fisted her hand around the gun, fingering the trigger. "Oh, I have," she said. "Every damn day. That's why I became an agent. But I don't know who has her. And if I took all my rage out on someone other than the person who did it, what would that accomplish? It would only make innocent people, other families, suffer the same way I did."

He snorted. "Innocent people," he scoffed. "Can I tell you something? I've been around a long time. Longer than you. And I've learned a lot in that time, but the thing I learned best is that no one is innocent. We're all guilty of something. Even you, Miss High and Mighty FBI Agent. We all have blood on our hands."

"That's not true."

"Oh, it is true!" he thundered. "And it's up to me to rid the world of the worst of the criminals. The ones who blatantly disregard the rules."

"All those people were doing was looking for a ride. They weren't your sister's killer."

"Yeah. How do you know that? The world is better off without them."

A red light flashed across her vision, painting itself on the back of the car seat. At first, she thought it was another car's tail lights, but then she heard the siren. She looked over her shoulder.

It was Michael. He was driving miraculously fast for once, keeping tight to the car's bumper, trying to edge closer to run him off the road.

"Looks like your friends are here," he said, glee in his voice. "Let's make this fun, shall we?"

He pressed harder on the gas, urging the car past 120.

Bracing herself against the back of the car as he swerved to and fro to avoid Michael, she steadied the gun, pointing it at him. The car swerved sharply into the grassy median, then out again. Then next time it swerved, it went into opposing traffic, swerving out just in time to avoid a head-on collision.

Heartbeat going mad, she shouted, "Pull the car over!"

"No way," he said calmly, twisting the wheel back and forth like a kid in a play vehicle. "I'm having too much fun."

They easily approached a semi, going slowly up a hill, hazard lights flashing. Just when Rylie was sure he was going to hit it head on, he swerved into the fast lane, nearly clipping its back end and forcing Michael, who was right behind, off the road.

As they sailed past the semi in record speed, it blared on its air horn.

I have to do something. And fast, she said, grabbing her phone. She texted Michael. *He's not pulling over. I'm going to have to do something drastic. Hang back.*

She wasn't sure if he'd get it, in the middle of the car chase, but if anything happened to her, at least they'd know that she'd tried to stop him.

Taking a deep breath, she aimed the gun at his head, ready to dive forward and take the wheel the second it went off.

Before she could squeeze the trigger, he flung his arm back, knocking the gun from her grip.

"You bitch," he snarled as she heard the gun hit the seat and bounce to the floor, skittering out of sight. She bent down to feel for it, but he splayed a hand on her face, shoving her back.

The second he did, the tires squealed and he lost control of the car. It veered off onto the medium, bumping over the uneven terrain.

When he spun to right the car, she lunged into the front seats, grabbing the wheel. He shoved her in the chest, trying to push her off, and her head slammed against the dashboard, and the gearshift poked between her ribs. She rolled off him, reaching again for the wheel, grabbing it from underneath and pulling herself up.

As she did, she slammed her body into his chest, shoulders first, her hands reaching for his eyes. She managed to get one finger into the gooey, viscous center of his eye socket and he let out a scream, pulling his foot from the gas.

Rylie tried to grab ahold of the steering wheel, but she was now wedged between it and her assailant, facing the back of the truck. "Off me! Get off me!" he shouted, shoving at her. But she had nowhere to go, sprawled out across the front row. By the time she turned to get a hand on the wheel, it was too late. The car was already careening for the guard rail.

She saw it advancing on them far too fast, and the only thing she could do was hold her breath, close her eyes, and brace herself.

The sickening crunch of metal upon metal sliced her eardrums, as the airbag released, the force hard against her head, shoving her face-first into the killer and toward the back of the car. She smashed into him as the car banked sharply to the left, skidding along the side of the rail. Though most of her vision was blurred by the night and the airbag, she could see the sparks flying, hear the squeal of the two metals rubbing against one another.

A moment later, when the car came to a juddering stop, she was finally able to pull herself upright, onto the front passenger seat.

"What—" Jeff started, his head lolling from side to side, his eyes closed. "What happened?"

Blinking away the double vision and pain in her head, she reached a hand down and found something familiar. Her gun.

As she picked it up, Jeff came to. "You bitch, look what you—"

Holding the gun by the barrel, she slammed it into the side of his head, and he fell forward immediately, onto the airbag. As she did, she thought of Moses Bedelbaum, the man whose roughing complaint Bill Matthews had advanced up the flagpole to get her in trouble. *Enjoy, Bill Matthews.*

"Don't call me that," she whispered, her every muscle aching in protest as she reached for the door handle. It took her three tries to actually open it and stumble out onto the shoulder of the road, but when she did, Michael was there to catch her.

"Ow," she said.

"Shit," he whispered as he reached for his phone. "I told you not to—"

"Maybe next time," she said with a small smile, "you should make me listen to you."

CHAPTER THIRTY ONE

Luckily, Rylie had gotten out of this latest altercation without having to visit the hospital. She was fine, except for a few bumps and bruises. Jeff had been brought in, and much was learned about him. His real name was Amos Farley, and he had been institutionalized most of his life. When he wasn't under medical care, he lived all alone outside of Missoula, in a compound littered with various cars, which he tinkered on as a hobby.

After the case was tied up, she and Michael returned to the police headquarters in Missoula. As they walked in, they were greeted with a round of applause.

Embarrassed, she tried to keep her head down, but Hoskins clapped her on the back. "I guess you're one of us, now, huh, Wolf?"

"I'm honored. But I couldn't have done it without my partner." She smiled over at Michael, who smiled back.

"Nah, it was all her," he said. "I was only there for clean-up."

"Hail the Daring Duo!" the others cried, gathering around them to give them thumbs-ups and fist-bumps.

Even Cooper Rich joined in. He'd taken up an office in the back to finish up his work, and must've heard the commotion, because he soon made his way to the center of the circle.

"Good job, Rylie," he said to her, his voice low. Had he meant to, or did he realize that his back was facing Michael, effectively closing him out? "I knew you'd get your man. You always do, somehow."

Michael's eyes rolled to the ceiling.

Right then, she was in such a good mood, she didn't even care if Michael and Cooper clashed. She didn't even care if Cooper went back to Bill Matthews and reported everything. She was perfectly happy, just being in the moment. "Thank you. When are you going back?"

He shrugged. "Still got a lot more work to do. Might be heading east instead. That where you're going?"

She stared in shock. He was going east? At first, she couldn't be sure she heard him right, but then Michael mumbled under his breath, "Surprise, surprise."

She nodded, wondering what kind of job would take him almost in lockstep with her travels. That meant she'd see him again, and the friction between him and her partner wouldn't be gone so easily. "Oh, that's nice."

"Yeah, so you're still on the hook for that dinner," he said with a wink, turning and walking off, practically nudging Michael out of the way as he did.

Oh, god. Why are men such testosterone-filled morons sometimes? Always fighting for Alpha.

"I think this calls for a late-night pizza party!" Hoskins called, and the office erupted into cheers. "Brizzy is paying!"

Louder cheers. Michael shook his head and shot each of them a look that said, *Really?*

"Okay, correction!" Hoskins shouted. "The chief is paying!"

"Better," he muttered, looking at Rylie, who laughed. "Are you sure you want to be one of us?"

"Yeah, I'm still thinking on that one."

Rylie and Michael walked together to the conference room, and when they got to the door, he stopped abruptly. There was no one else around. She thought he was going to reach forward and open the door, but instead, the direction of his reach went a different way, right for her cheek. The pad of his thumb rubbed there.

Her eyes must've widened because he said, "Little blood."

"Oh. Not mine."

"Good. Sure you don't want to go to the hospital and get checked out? You could have a concussion."

She shook her head. "If I do, they'd tell me to do what I'm going to do anyway. Rest."

He snorted. "Yeah. You, rest? We all know that's not happening."

She laughed. "Okay. You've got me. Maybe not. Resting makes me antsy." She shrugged. "I was thinking we could stop at my father's place on the way back? The last time, I got chewed out for not being a good enough daughter, so I promised myself I'd visit him more than once a decade. In Cody, Wyoming."

He nodded. "Sure. Why not?"

He eyed her for a while, and she could almost see the unspoken question hovering in a thought-bubble over his head. *And you're also going to want to stop in Story Creek on the way back, aren't you?* But for whatever reason, he didn't say it. Maybe it was because the mood was light and celebratory, and he didn't want to ruin it. Instead, he said, "You've got guts, girl."

She rolled her eyes. "Blah blah blah. What I really have is a hankering for pizza. I'm starving. I bet you can eat an entire pie yourself, can't you?"

He nodded. "That's one challenge I know I'm up for."

*

Rylie and Michael exchanged nonstop flirtation and witty banter on the way down to her hometown of Cody, Wyoming, but as they drew closer, she became quieter and quieter, more and more tense.

It wasn't the town of Cody. Cody hadn't changed much since she was a little girl. There was the same barbecue place on the corner, the same car dealership, selling old hunks of junk. Her own house was out of the city proper, and they didn't go past it. Rylie wasn't ready for that, and wasn't ready to explain to Michael what her life had been like after her mother died and Maren disappeared. It had been the bleakest nine years of her life, and she shuddered with the thought of it.

She pulled into the apartment complex, next to her father's red Ford Ranger. It hadn't moved since the last time she'd been there, and was parked perfectly in the spot, with almost military precision. Her father was neat, that way.

She glared at it as she got out of her truck. Michael started to get out, too, but she said, "You don't have to come. I won't be long."

"What, are you kidding me? Of course I'm coming."

Of course he was. It was silly to suggest otherwise. Michael Brisbane lived for meet-and-greets. It was his favorite thing to do.

The apartment complex was a two-story building with brown paneled walls and mustard-colored doors. Modern, probably, about thirty years ago. But now, it looked as if it'd definitely seen better days. The paint was peeling on most of the doors and there were grills, bicycles, sporting equipment, and unsightly lawn chairs on the balconies. The last time she'd come here, she knew her father's place at once, because his balcony was the only one that was absolutely spotless. That was her dad.

Michael following close behind, she climbed the stairs and went to the door.

Rick Wolf was just as handsome as ever, tall, with dark hair and piercing blue eyes. There was more salt than pepper in his beard now, and his belly filled out his trademark flannel shirt more fully. There were more trademark scars of his heavy drinking there, too—his eyes were bleary, his face bloated, with broken blood vessels dotting his nose. Just as he had the last time she'd paid him a visit a few weeks ago, he looked utterly mystified at her appearance there.

"Rylie," he said stiffly. "Why are you here?"

She'd been asking herself the same question. But after talking with her father-figure Hal Buxton, she'd decided that her father still cared. Why else would he have called Hal a couple weeks ago, asking about her? He and Hal had never gotten along. Despite her father's icy treatment of her, when she'd heard that he had been asking about her, she knew he wasn't too far gone. If she was going to peel through the layers of resentment to get to the part of him that still felt something for her, she had to try.

So as hard as it was, as much as being with him brought back those terrible memories, she forced a smile. "Hi, Dad. You said last time I stayed away too long. So here I am. *Not* staying away."

He swallowed, contemplating this, then his eyes shifted behind her, toward where her partner was standing, and narrowed slightly.

She pulled him forward. Maybe his legendary charm could dispel the awkwardness of the moment. "Uh, this is Michael Brisbane. My partner."

Michael extended his hand. "Pleased to meet you."

Rick Wolf looked at his hand for a long time before barely shaking it. "Partner? Is that what they call husbands these days?"

"He's my partner *in the FBI,*" she clarified, noting Michael's amused look. "Remember? I'm an agent?"

He wiped his nose and sniffed. "Huh. Still single? You're getting too old to be single."

She kept the smile up as best she could, even though she could feel it cracking. "Thanks, Dad," she said. "Can we come in?"

He nodded and stepped aside. Though he might have had a bit of a drinking problem ever since her mother's death, he still kept the place clean and spartan. He motioned to a leather sofa, and they both sat down. "I can get you something? Beer? Crackers?"

Rylie shook her head. Michael picked up a framed photograph, one of the few items of décor he had in the room. "No thanks," Michael said. "This is impressive."

Her father grabbed a beer from the fridge, flipped off the cap, took a swig, and nodded. "Ain't it?"

She watched Michael set it down, wondering if he truly cared about fishing. Or if he saw the glaring dysfunction in their family dynamic. It wasn't hard to spot. That photograph wasn't of her, or anyone else in the family. It was from a time he'd gone fishing upstate and caught a giant bass. In the photograph, he was almost smiling. Almost. She'd never seen him smile before, especially over something she did.

Her father sat down in the recliner across from them, one so old that it had his shape worn into the upholstery. He said, "You a fisherman, Mike?"

Michael nodded. "Sure am."

Well, that answered that question. She couldn't help it, but it knocked Michael down a couple of pegs on her respect scale. She knew it wasn't fair. She'd liked fishing once, too, until she realized her dad loved it more than her.

Rylie watched them chat, smiling as they talked about all the fish they'd caught. As usual, Michael worked his charming ways and put her father at ease in a way she'd never been able to. Even if her father wasn't speaking directly to her, he seemed relaxed and okay. She decided it was a successful visit, one more step on the long road to healing their relationship.

She reached her hand into her pocket, turning Maren's necklace over in her fingers, feeling the chain and the sharp points of the initial. She didn't want to ruin this visit by telling her father about it.

CHAPTER THIRTY TWO

Rylie's mood during the ride back east was somber. She played music too loud on the radio, hoping that would discourage Michael from trying to talk about it.

It didn't work. About an hour into the drive, he turned down the radio and said, "So, your dad's a nice guy."

She grunted.

"What does that mean?"

"Like I told you, after my sister disappeared and my mom was murdered, we really didn't get along." She shrugged. "Actually, I don't really know if we got along before that. I was young. And the rest of my family had served as a buffer. When it was just us, it was… hard."

The understatement to end all understatements. But she didn't want to go into it.

"Well, he seems pretty nice."

She glanced over at him and had to smile. "You think everyone is nice."

"Not true."

"Oh, yes it is. You get along with just about everyone."

"Nah. I did not think that guy who killed all the hitchhikers was a nice man."

She snorted. "Oh. One. In a country of four hundred million. Amazing." She shook her head at his confused expression—how could he deny it? Everyone loved him, and he loved everyone else. "Actually, I think if you had met that killer on the road and hadn't known he was a killer, you'd have probably liked him, too. He seemed pretty normal. You'd probably have been best—"

"Where are you going?"

She paused. Inadvertently—okay, not so inadvertently—she'd driven off the interstate, toward the sign that said Elephant Hole. She'd been thinking about it in the back of her head the whole time, so much so that she just expected that was where they were going. She'd forgotten that he still thought they were going home.

"Oh, well—"

He spoke over her. "I get it, I get it. You want to see what's there."

"Yeah, well. While we're in the neighborhood, I thought we should—"

"You don't need to explain. Let's go. I'm ready." He rubbed his hands together.

She smiled. What would she have done without him?

Nothing, she realized. If it hadn't been for him, she never would've found the necklace in the first place. So if anyone deserved to be here while she looked for clues, it was him. "We'll only be here a few minutes, and then we can get on our way—"

"Hey. I told you. No rush."

"Well, I'm sure you want to be back before it gets late—"

"For what? My adoring public? So I don't turn into a pumpkin?" He ran a hand through his hair. "Come on. It's fine."

Her heart pattered in her chest. The only men who'd ever been so nice to her were Hal Buxton, her neighbor, and Joe, her ex. They'd looked out for her. And it felt like Michael was doing the same thing. But there was something different about him. A feeling she didn't want to explore… She'd seen the way he acted around Cooper Rich, and hadn't bothered entertaining it, but a part of her had definitely wished that he'd been acting possessive of her, not just because she was his partner, but because… well, he cared about her.

Because she was definitely starting to care about him. Definitely.

Pushing away those thoughts, she followed the signs to Elephant Hole.

She'd heard about the place. It was a nineteenth-century military outpost, famed for battles between native tribes and the US cavalry. George Custer was said to have been stationed there. But that was the story of most of the monuments in the area, and growing up close by, she hadn't paid much attention to them. Now, as she drove in, she looked around, wondering just what she could find in this place that would still remain, after twenty years.

There was a small log cabin with a giant flagpole in front, American and Wyoming flags, flapping in the harsh wind. Not a single car parked in the lot. A sign in the window said, CLOSED. The paper that had come with the necklace had said *Elephant Hole Well.* That could've been anywhere.

"What do you think?" she asked as she pulled into the lot and cut the engine. "You think there's a well somewhere around here?"

"Let's just take a little hike. Maybe we'll find one."

He went to the back of the truck and took out his backpack with their tactical equipment, bottles of water, and other essentials. She stepped out onto the curb, and they walked along the asphalt path, which was bordered on each side by yellow grass, as far as the eye could see. There were a few trees here and there, and dark brown mountains rising into the distance. She didn't see anything resembling a well, but it had to be here. "It's probably hidden."

"Which is probably a good thing—you wouldn't find any evidence if twenty years of tourists have been all over it."

They walked out into the grass, following dirt paths that seemed to lead in all directions from the cabin, like fingers from a hand. As they wandered, she thought about Maren in this field. What had she been doing? Who had she been with? She'd been brought there against her will. What had caused her to lose her necklace? Had she taken it off and left it there as a clue?

That's something Maren would've done. She was always the more clever one.

Maybe, though, this was where they took her to die. Maybe they'd killed her by that well.

She shook off the terrible thought, just as Michael called to her. "Wolf!"

She broke out of her trance to find him standing several hundred feet away, staring at something in the ground.

At his call, her knees went weak. Had he found something? For a moment, she thought he was just going to call her over to some interesting find that had nothing to do with her situation—an old arrowhead, maybe. There were thousands of them buried around here. But as she moved closer, she saw the look on his face. He was concerned.

She'd intended to go back down the path she'd taken, instead of taking a direct line to where he stood, but when she saw the alarm in her face, she cut across the tall grass, which slapped the legs of her jeans as she ran, faster and faster.

"What?" she called, breathless, as she came upon it.

There was an area in the ground nearly covered by grass. Around it was orange utility fencing, but in the center of it was a circular wooden cover, so old it was rotting away. A sign on the fencing said *WELL—DANGER—KEEP OUT.*

This was it. Either Maren had been here, or her killers had, or someone had brought the necklace here. She wasn't sure what the connection was to this place, but she'd just taken a giant step forward in solving the mystery. She was not going to back out now.

Without a second thought, she stepped over the yellow fencing. Then she went to the wooden cover, lifted the metal latch, and tugged. It moved, just barely. "Help me."

"Wait, what are you doing?"

"What does it look like I'm doing?" she said, pulling harder.

"But—what are you expecting to find in there?"

She stopped and glared at him. He looked really worried now. "Not my sister's bones. Is that what you're worried about? I'm sure, if they found the necklace here way back when, this was the first place they would've checked. But maybe there's something else that can help us."

He nodded, came forward, and easily helped her lug the heavy cover aside. She peered in. After a few feet, it descended into blackness. She grabbed her phone, turned on the flashlight, and pointed it down the shaft.

There wasn't much to see. It went about twenty feet, and the bottom seemed to be nothing but dust.

"Can you lower me in?" she asked.

He stared at her. "Yeah—but are you sure?"

"Of course. I didn't come all the way out here not to make a full search of the place. And I'm not leaving until every stone near this well is unturned."

His lips twisted. "What happened to *We'll only be a few minutes…*"

"That was before you found the well. Now, I need to go in there. If you want to wait in the car…"

"No, no, no. That's not what I'm saying." He dropped his backpack and pulled out a rope. Uncoiling it, he tied it to a metal pipe in the ground and gave it a good tug. "Sure you can—"

"Of course." She was already grabbing the rope, lowering herself down. "Just keep the light on me, all right?"

It wound up being harder than she thought. She'd had climbing drills in the academy, but she'd been younger then. The area was dusty and enclosed, and even with the flashlight's glow, everything was in a haze. She sneezed several times as she lowered herself down. Finally, when she was a few feet from the bottom, she jumped and landed in the soft, grainy earth.

There wasn't an ounce of moisture down there. The well had been dry for quite some time. She grabbed her own flashlight and shone it on the brick walls of the well, looking for anything of use. Then she kicked around the dirt, in case anything had been buried.

When she was about to give up, her foot hit against something hard.

She reached down and touched it. It was smooth and cold, and too large to pull out. She started digging around, trying to free the thing, and before she'd even gotten it out, she knew what it was.

It was a mirror, cracked from one side to the next.

"I found something," she called up, her voice echoing in the enclosed space.

"What?"

She wasn't sure. Why would a mirror be down here? Who had thrown it down here? As she cleared it more and more, she realized it was a rearview mirror from someone's car. She handled it gently, even though it was unlikely that there'd be old fingerprints on it. But she'd heard stranger things. Slipping it into the pocket of her jacket, she grabbed the rope and gave it a tug.

"I'm done here. You can pull me up."

She scrambled up the rope, and when she emerged from the well, she showed him what she'd found. "It's probably nothing," she said doubtfully, as they walked back to the truck. "But I still have to try."

"Hey, you never know. All it takes is one little piece of evidence. It might be everything. The thing that cracks the case wide open."

He was right. Older cold cases had been solved on a lot less.

And as she tilted the mirror into the light, she could've sworn she saw the whorls and ridges of a fingerprint. Blinking, she looked again, sure she was seeing things. But the more she tilted it and looked, the clearer it became.

Maybe it was just her mind playing tricks on her. Wishful thinking. But she had to believe that there was still some hope in Maren's case. She was the only one on Earth who was still looking for her sister, and she needed to keep that fire going, even when all the other ones had burned out.

EPILOGUE

Cooper Rich had traded in his rental car for the trip out east. Now, he leaned his rented motorcycle against the side of the cabin and watched Michael Brisbane standing out in the field, looking down.

What the hell were they up to? He could only guess.

He still felt terrible, playing spy. This was wrong. The wrong way to go about getting a promotion. But other than his job, what else did he have in life to be proud of? Nothing. His life was being an FBI agent. It was his entire identity, the thing that meant the most to him.

So what if he had to lie to Rylie Wolf a little in order to rise in the ranks? In every operation, there were casualties. Risks. He needed to weigh them. Rylie was a fighter. She'd probably land on her feet no matter what he found out.

But she'd also probably hate him forever.

The thought was still tangling his gut when his phone buzzed with a text. It was from Bill Matthews: *Dammit. Keep on it Rich. FOLLOW HER. I want to know everything she's up to.*

He sighed. When he signed up for the FBI, this was the last goddamn thing he'd wanted to do. He'd never minded surveillance, but spying on one of his own? It was dirty.

And Rylie might have screwed things up from time to time, but the bottom line was, she got things done. Case in point, this last crime with the murdered hitchhikers. She'd gone in, gotten her hands dirty, and taken the bull by the horns, like always. Sure, her methods had been unorthodox, but they worked. Pure and simple.

The Missoula police had been thrilled. They would've pinned a medal on her if she'd stayed around long enough to collect it. Even the chief of police had said that if it weren't for Rylie Wolf, there was no doubt that the killer would still be out there. That incompetent pretty boy Michael Brisbane didn't have the stuff. Rylie Wolf had led that operation.

When he'd sent news of that to Bill Matthews, of course he was upset. That was probably the last thing the man wanted to hear.

And that was why this assignment was bullshit. A wild goose chase. Maybe Matthews had sent him out here because he was gunning to get rid of him, too. Rich had gotten too close to the enemy, and now Matthews wanted them both gone. Maybe the talk of promotion was all bullshit.

As he leaned against the log cabin and removed his sunglasses to peer across the plain, Rylie suddenly appeared, the wind tossing her dark hair around her shoulders. She was pretty. Loyal as hell. Braver than anyone. He'd always wanted to ask her out, but he'd been afraid she'd laugh in his face and he'd never live it down. He hadn't been lying when he said he'd wanted to see her again.

If only he hadn't been lying about the rest of it. If she found out the truth, she'd tear off his balls and feed them to him.

From his hiding spot behind the cabin, he watched as the two of them walked back to the truck. Rylie was holding something in her hand, which she dropped into her pocket as they walked. He wondered what it was.

"It's probably nothing," she was saying. "But I still have to try."

"Hey, you never know. All it takes is one little piece of evidence. It might be everything. The thing that cracks the case wide open."

Another case? What was that all about?

Wait… she'd mentioned something once before. Way back when they were in the academy together, and they'd been asked why they wanted to become agents. She'd said something about a sister. It had happened a long time ago. Decades, maybe. A murder? And it had happened around here, too. This was where Rylie was from. She'd grown up somewhere around here, so it was entirely possible the murder had happened here, too.

Right… the sister. Even though she never spoke of it after that day, he'd always gotten the feeling she'd been hung up on it, that she was battling demons she couldn't seem to get past, without knowing what had really happened.

So maybe that was what she was chasing here. Maybe that was the one silver lining in her being sent back out here—that she could finally confront those demons.

And now, she'd just found a clue that would bring her closer. Good for her.

As Rylie Wolf and her pretty-boy partner pulled away, leaving Cooper alone at Elephant Hole, he pulled out his phone and sent a text to Bill Williams: *I think she's looking into a cold case. The murder of her sister. And she just found a big piece of evidence. I don't know what.*

A moment later, Bill Matthews texted back: *Her sister was murdered?*

Cooper Rich snorted. The guy had about as much tact as a cardboard box. No wonder no one on the staff liked him. He never bothered to get to know anyone on a personal basis. They were all cattle to him; he was too important for the people who worked under him.

He replied: *Yeah. I think. Or kidnapped. Like twenty years ago. But she's always been looking for who did it.*

When he sent it, he figured it was pretty innocuous. It was a valiant thing, to want to uncover a long-held family mystery, to put it to rest and find closure. He admired her for it. There was nothing Bill Matthews could say against that.

But then the text from Bill came in: *I think I can use that.*

He wheeled his motorcycle out to the road, frowning and wondering just what he'd inadvertently set in motion. Bill had already moved Rylie halfway across the country. He'd already tried to get her fired. He'd done a hell of a lot to her.

But clearly not enough.

So as he straddled his bike and headed east, one question lingered in Cooper Rich's mind: *What is that weasel going to do to Rylie Wolf now?*

NOW AVAILABLE!

TAKE YOU
(A Rylie Wolf FBI Suspense Thriller—Book 5)

On a stretch of highway in the Pacific Northwest known for the country's highest number of serial killers, cold cases pile up across state lines, stumping the local police. An elite FBI unit is formed, with brilliant special agent Rylie Wolf at its head—and this time Rylie is summoned to a lonely stretch of highway where active and cold cases converge. Has an old killer re-surfaced?

Or is this the work of someone new?

"Molly Black has written a taut thriller that will keep you on the edge of your seat… I absolutely loved this book and can't wait to read the next book in the series!"
—Reader review for Girl One: Murder

A complex psychological crime thriller full of twists and turns and packed with heart-pounding suspense, the RYLIE WOLF mystery series will make you fall in love with a brilliant new female protagonist and keep you turning pages late into the night. It is a perfect addition for fans of Robert Dugoni, Rachel Caine, Melinda Leigh or Mary Burton.

Book #6 in the series—DARE YOU—is now also available.

"I binge read this book. It hooked me in and didn't stop till the last few pages… I look forward to reading more!"
—Reader review for Found You

"I loved this book! Fast-paced plot, great characters and interesting insights into investigating cold cases. I can't wait to read the next book!"

—Reader review for Girl One: Murder

"Very good book… You will feel like you are right there looking for the kidnapper! I know I will be reading more in this series!"
—Reader review for Girl One: Murder

"This is a very well written book and holds your interest from page 1… Definitely looking forward to reading the next one in the series, and hopefully others as well!"
—Reader review for Girl One: Murder

"Wow, I cannot wait for the next in this series. Starts with a bang and just keeps going."
—Reader review for Girl One: Murder

"Well written book with a great plot, one that will keep you up at night. A page turner!"
—Reader review for Girl One: Murder

"A great suspense that keeps you reading… can't wait for the next in this series!"
—Reader review for Found You

"Sooo soo good! There are a few unforeseen twists… I binge read this like I binge watch Netflix. It just sucks you in."
—Reader review for Found You

Molly Black

Bestselling author Molly Black is author of the MAYA GRAY FBI suspense thriller series, comprising nine books (and counting); of the RYLIE WOLF FBI suspense thriller series, comprising six books (and counting); of the TAYLOR SAGE FBI suspense thriller series, comprising six books (and counting); and of the KATIE WINTER FBI suspense thriller series, comprising nine books (and counting).

An avid reader and lifelong fan of the mystery and thriller genres, Molly loves to hear from you, so please feel free to visit www.mollyblackauthor.com to learn more and stay in touch.

BOOKS BY MOLLY BLACK

MAYA GRAY MYSTERY SERIES
GIRL ONE: MURDER (Book #1)
GIRL TWO: TAKEN (Book #2)
GIRL THREE: TRAPPED (Book #3)
GIRL FOUR: LURED (Book #4)
GIRL FIVE: BOUND (Book #5)
GIRL SIX: FORSAKEN (Book #6)
GIRL SEVEN: CRAVED (Book #7)
GIRL EIGHT: HUNTED (Book #8)
GIRL NINE: GONE (Book #9)

RYLIE WOLF FBI SUSPENSE THRILLER
FOUND YOU (Book #1)
CAUGHT YOU (Book #2)
SEE YOU (Book #3)
WANT YOU (Book #4)
TAKE YOU (Book #5)
DARE YOU (Book #6)

TAYLOR SAGE FBI SUSPENSE TIIRILLER
DON'T LOOK (Book #1)
DON'T BREATHE (Book #2)
DON'T RUN (Book #3)
DON'T FLINCH (Book #4)
DON'T REMEMBER (Book #5)
DON'T TELL (Book #6)

KATIE WINTER FBI SUSPENSE THRILLER
SAVE ME (Book #1)
REACH ME (Book #2)
HIDE ME (Book #3)
BELIEVE ME (Book #4)
HELP ME (Book #5)
FORGET ME (Book #6)

HOLD ME (Book #7)
PROTECT ME (Book #8)
REMEMBER ME (Book #9)